W9-ASZ-104

Reel Life
STARRING US

LISA GREENWALD

AMULET BOOKS

NEW YORK

Reel Life
STARRING US

PUBLISHER'S NOTE: This is a work of fiction. Names, characters, places, and incidents are either the product of the author's imagination or are used fictitiously, and any resemblance to actual persons, living or dead, business establishments, events, or locales is entirely coincidental.

The Library of Congress has catalogued the hardcover edition of this book as follows:

Greenwald, Lisa.
Reel life starring us / Lisa Greenwald.
p. cm.
Summary: Dina is used to being popular but starting a new school in eighth grade is difficult, especially where cliques rule, and although working with "queen bee" Chelsea on a video project should help, Chelsea is hiding huge family problems that could mean trouble for both girls.
ISBN: 978-1-4197-0026-2
[1. Popularity—Fiction. 2. Middle schools—Fiction. 3. Schools—Fiction.
4. Video recording—Fiction. 5. Secrets—Fiction. 6. Family life—New York
(State)—Long Island—Fiction. 7. Moving, Household—Fiction. 8. Long Island
(N.Y.)—Fiction.] I. Title.
PZ7.G85199Ree 2011
[Fic]—dc23
2011015079

Paperback ISBN: 978-1-4197-0426-0

Text copyright © 2011 Lisa Greenwald
Book design by Chad W. Beckerman

Originally published in hardcover in 2011 by Amulet Books, an imprint of ABRAMS. This edition published in 2013. All rights reserved. No portion of this book may be reproduced, stored in a retrieval system, or transmitted in any form or by any means, mechanical, electronic, photocopying, recording, or otherwise, without written permission from the publisher. Amulet Books and Amulet Paperbacks are registered trademarks of Harry N. Abrams, Inc.

Printed and bound in U.S.A.
10 9 8 7 6 5 4 3 2 1

Amulet Books are available at special discounts when purchased in quantity for premiums and promotions as well as fundraising or educational use. Special editions can also be created to specification. For details, contact specialsales@abramsbooks.com or the address below.

ABRAMS

THE ART OF BOOKS SINCE 1949

115 West 18th Street
New York, NY 10011
www.abramsbooks.com

FOR MY BUBBIE AND ZEYDA,

HELEN AND ALLYN GREENWALD:

GRANDPARENTS,

CHEERLEADERS,

AND PUBLICISTS

DINA

Video tip: Use an L-cut—introduce a scene with an audio cue a second or two before the scene actually starts.

I'm standing in the second-floor bathroom, shaking crunched-up potato chips from the bottom of my backpack into the garbage can.

Anywhere else potato chips are considered good—delicious, even.

Here it doesn't seem to be that way.

This whole starting-a-new-school thing would be easier if I had a T-shirt that stated the truth, or a removable tattoo on my forehead, or something, just so people would know: I was cool at my old school. Really, I was. Yeah, it was a private school with fifty kids in the grade. Everyone was artsy in his or her own way. And it wasn't very cliquey. But I was cool. People liked me.

Shouldn't it be automatic that if I was *someone* there, I'd be *someone* here, too?

"Chipped already?" the girl at the sink asks me. "On your first day?"

"So it's, like, a thing?" I ask her. She looks at me, confused. "Being chipped, I mean?"

"What do you mean it's 'like, a thing'?" she asks, shaking her hands dry.

"I don't get it. I almost thought it was an accident that all these chips landed in my backpack." I pick the last few remaining chip crumbs out of the zipper.

"Nope. You were chipped. Someone saw you and decided that you were a good target." She takes one last look in the mirror and smoothes out the sides of her hair. "Good luck."

See, if I had the shirt, I wouldn't have been chipped. It would be known. If you were cool in your old school, you're cool in your new school, too.

I leave the bathroom and go to gym. I'm waiting in the bleachers, looking around to see if I can find the culprit—the person who chipped me.

Does anyone have a smug look on her face? Is anyone glaring at me?

So far, no. No one even notices me.

It's hard to concentrate on this because everyone's sneakers are making that annoying rubbing sound against the floor. Ms. Berger, the gym teacher, blows her whistle every other second, which is way more often than she needs to.

We're playing badminton, not basketball. I don't know why anyone needs a whistle for badminton. I haven't even played yet. I've been sitting in the bleachers this whole time.

And that's when I notice her. Three rows below me. She's probably not the one who chipped me. She has too many other things going on to do that. She's the one who's surrounded by her best friends, the one who's happy and confident. The one who just loves school.

That's where I should be sitting. With her. Chelsea Stern.

Her friends have a cheer for her. "Go, Sea-Sea! Go, Stern! Go-go, Sea-Sea Stern!"

They keep saying it. It's catchy. I almost join in, just because that's what happens when I hear something over and over again. It'll echo in my head for the rest of the day.

I turn my attention back to the gym floor. I've never seen anyone take badminton as seriously as everyone does here. To be honest, the only badminton games I've ever seen were in the backyards of Sheffield, where I used to live. The nets drooped; we hit the birdie only every tenth shot or so. People usually got bored of the game after about five minutes.

But here badminton is a real sport.

"Dina Gross, you're up!" Ms. Berger calls, looking all around for me. The way this gym class is structured, only eight people actually participate at any given time. It doesn't seem like people really build up a sweat.

Chelsea's friends look at me. They don't smile. Were they the people who did it? The *chippers*?

"Do you play tennis?" the girl I'm playing against, one of Chelsea's friends, asks me as I'm bending down to pick up the badminton racket.

"Not really," I say. "You?"

"Yeah, so does mostly everyone. That's why we're bizarrely good at this sport." She smiles. "You kind of look weirded out."

I don't understand how she can tell that. But she's right. "Well, yeah, a little, I guess."

The girl serves and I swing. Of course I don't get it over the net—because going that fast, the birdie is impossible to hit.

"Good game," she says after clearly beating me. And beating me bad.

In the locker room, when we're changing back into our regular clothes, I keep a careful watch on my backpack. Maybe the secret is that you never leave your backpack unattended, like you can't leave bags unattended at an airport.

There should be a rule book for this kind of stuff. Something I could follow so I could avoid more potato chip incidents.

After gym, I'm walking to my next class when I notice more. More chipping. Kids emptying their bags of crumbs.

How do the kids here even have that many bags of potato chips? Where do they store them? And why do they want to waste them dumping them into other people's bags when they could be eating that crunchy deliciousness?

It's all over the place. When the person's not looking, when the person is looking. Bags left in the hallway, bags on people's shoulders.

There's no rhyme or reason.

It just keeps happening.

I'm tempted to take out my camera and record this. I could e-mail the video to Ali and show her what things are like here. She'll never believe me if I don't.

So I take out my camera. No one really knows me yet anyway. I could be some foreign exchange student who's never coming back, for all they know. I could be some kind of undercover reporter doing a story for the local news.

I could be shooting a movie about middle school. Some guy in Korea shot a whole movie on his iPhone. I would try that too if my parents were nice enough to buy me one.

As I'm walking to social studies, I shoot videos of this whole potato chip thing.

People don't really notice me. They just say "Oh, man," and "Ugggh, again," and "Seriously? That's the third time this week." And then the person who did the chipping just laughs and walks away.

Does the principal know about this? The teachers?

No one gets hurt, really, so it's not the worst thing ever. But it's messy. It took me twenty minutes to get all the crumbs out just now and I'm not even sure I got all of them.

And it's a waste of perfectly delicious chips, too.

These aren't the no-frills brand you find in gigantic bags in the grocery store. These kids are using every brand you've ever heard of: Kettle chips and "Dirty" chips and Baked Lay's. Barbecue. Salt and vinegar. Olive oil. Every kind of potato chip in the universe.

So I keep videoing, and I'll admit some people are looking at me strangely. Like, who's this girl who's just going around videoing stuff?

But it's weird—this whole chipping thing. I want to figure it out.

And it's not like anyone's talking to me, so what else do I have to do?

2

CHELSEA

Sasha Preston piece of advice: Stand up straight;
people will take you more seriously that way.

How many times have I heard someone say, "Every cloud has a silver lining"? Probably a billion. I've always thought it was the cheesiest thing ever, but it's actually kind of true when you think about it.

I thought that missing the first month of eighth grade because of mono was going to be the worst thing ever, but in reality, it wasn't that bad. My friends e-mailed me the homework and kept me updated on all the latest gossip through texts and video chats. My mom brought me make-your-own salads from Bagel Bonanza every day for lunch. Well, up until about a week ago she did; then she said she could make them just as good at home. She really can't, though; the avocado is never ripe enough.

But that doesn't matter because I'm back at school now. And now that I'm better, the whole day is like a huge welcome back party for me.

The best part of being home all that time was that it helped me keep my secret. Now that I'm back in school, it's going to be much harder to do, but I think I can. I mean, I don't have a choice, so I *know* I can.

The longer you keep a secret, the more it just becomes a part of you, something you carefully guard and protect. The longer you keep a secret, the more you start to believe that whatever you're hiding really isn't true.

I've kept it this long and I'm not giving up.

Mr. Valakis walks into social studies and snaps me out of my thoughts. He's one of those teachers that everyone talks about. Either you love him or you hate him, but either way, you talk about him.

I don't really get it, though; he seems like any old teacher to me. Gray beard, short-sleeve button-down: exactly like you'd picture a social studies teacher, as if he stepped out of a TV show. Like Sasha Preston's show, *Sasha Says So*. It's my favorite, and her teachers are all like Mr. Valakis.

It feels good to be back at school, sitting with my friends and not thinking about things at home. Kendall and Molly are on each side of me, and every few seconds they put their arms around me. "We're soooo glad you're back," Kendall says over and over again.

She means it, too. They need me. We're a group of three, and what's a group of three without the third? Or maybe I'm the first, not the third. Either way, a group of three needs three people, obviously.

And we're the best group of three that ever existed.

A millisecond after the bell rings, Mr. Valakis gets order in the classroom without even trying. We all stop talking immediately; he's that kind of teacher.

"We have two new students today. Well, new to our class. Only one is new to our school. Please welcome Dina and Chelsea. And please get to work on your fiftieth-anniversary projects while I get them situated."

He gestures us over to his desk.

I wave good-bye to Kendall and Molly, even though I'm not really going all that far.

"Chelsea, I see you're not really new to the school, just a little late to eighth grade." He smiles at us both. "So how are you settling in so far?"

"Fine," I say.

"Dina?" he looks to the new girl, who doesn't really seem to be paying attention.

"Oh, um . . . great." She laughs, even though nothing's funny.

He swivels himself forward in his desk chair and starts moving some papers around. I think he's the kind of person who needs to do at least two things at a time. "How familiar are you with the fiftieth-anniversary gala?"

"I read my mom's e-mail, so I know a little about it." After I say it, I immediately feel like a weirdo. What kid reads their mom's e-mail? Only obsessive worriers like me, but I try not to think about that. "It's in December, right?"

"Yes. Well, I'll get both of you up to speed. Dina, do you know much about this? I know it's only your first day here at Rockwood Hills."

"I don't know anything." She laughs again. "I mean, about this."

I can't really get a good read on this girl. She's new, today's her first day, but she's a month late starting. It's strange that we're both late and starting the same day. We seem to be grouped together into some latecomers club or something.

She's got an artsy look—long curly hair, flared corduroy pants, trapezoid-shaped brown chunky glasses. She's plain, but not because she's lazy about her appearance, but because she wants to look that way. And she's smiling, even now, smiling and laughing for no reason whatsoever. She's the kind of girl that teachers just *loooove* and most kids hate except for the select few who find her intriguing.

I have her figured out already.

Mr. Valakis is still explaining the gala. "Okay, here's the scoop. It's Rockwood Hills Middle School's fiftieth anniversary this year, so the PTA is organizing a huge gala event. Black tie, yada yada. The eighth graders all have a role in it. The science fair projects will be displayed, the chorus is singing, there's a little play parody thing being worked on, and some kids are painting murals. Pretty much anything and everything is going into this event."

I turn around to look at my friends. They're in the back row working on whatever they're working on, and they actually look serious about it. Why didn't they tell me about this? They told me about everything else—like, how they couldn't stop cracking up because Brynn Waverly slipped on a mound of mashed potatoes in the cafeteria one day and how pretty much everyone failed the first math test of the year, so Ms. McGinnis let them retake it.

But they didn't tell me anything about this. Maybe it's not that big of a deal. But if it is that big of a deal, I should have known what they were doing for it. I could've been working on it at home this whole month.

"So you're a little late to be starting this, and I doubt you had much time to think about it, but any ideas on what you'd like to contribute?" He looks at me first.

"I can just go join my friends in the back, help them with whatever they're working on." I smile and stand up straight. I hate that I slouch so much, and teachers always want kids to have good posture.

That's easy enough. For a second, I thought he was going to pair me up with the new girl or something. I guess now that we're in eighth grade we don't have to be paired up with people anymore and we can choose who we want to work with.

Mr. Valakis keeps clicking his pen open and closed, and it's starting to drive me crazy. I want him to give me the okay so I can go back and work with my friends and things can just go back to normal as quickly as possible. How many more times is he going to say that I'm starting school late? I know I'm late. Sheesh.

"That's a possibility," he says. "But we'd really like it to be something you're interested in." He waits a few seconds, and when I don't say anything, he looks at Dina. "Before class, I saw you playing with one of those little video cameras," he says to her.

"Oh, yeah." She laughs again. I swear, this girl laughs at anything. What's wrong with her? "I'm kind of obsessed with recording things. I just keep it in my bag."

Mr. Valakis nods, and I begin to get a bad feeling about this whole thing. Why isn't he letting me go in the back and work with my friends?

"Well, there's an idea!" He sounds a little too excited. "A video! You can do something like 'A Day in the Life of a Rockwood Hills Student.'"

"Oh, um, well, that'd be cool . . . but I just got here," Dina says. "So I don't know much about the school, obviously." She scratches her head, looking like she's in pain. "But, I mean, I could try and, um . . . yeah."

There are times when you do something you really, really don't mean to. But it just happens, totally out of your control. This is one of those times.

I laugh.

I crack up, even though I don't really want to or mean to, but it's just the way she was talking, rambling really, until a lightbulb went off in her brain and she realized she should be nice and respectful to this teacher.

Mr. Valakis looks at me, not pleased at all, and Dina steps back a few feet, twirling a strand of hair so tight around her finger.

"No problem, Dina. Chelsea here can—and will—help you with the video!" Mr. Valakis claps and the whole class looks up, which makes this whole thing seem even worse. Just a second ago, wasn't I going to work with my friends on whatever they were working on? How did things change so drastically so fast? "Right, Chelsea?"

"I thought I was gonna work with Kendall and Molly," I say as quietly and as politely as possible. "I'm really interested in their project."

Liar, liar, pants on fire. I don't even know what the project is, but I'm hoping Mr. Valakis doesn't know that!

Dina's looking at the floor like she's counting the little specs on the hideous green linoleum tile.

"You'll do great with the video," Mr. Valakis says. "You'll show Dina the ropes. With her video skills and your knowledge of Rockwood Hills Middle School, this is going to be superb."

Both of us are silent.

"Now get to work," he says.

Dina nods, a little reluctant and a little enthusiastic, a combination that seems impossible, really. Then she walks back to her desk and I start to follow her.

"Chelsea," Mr. Valakis says, catching me before I walk away. "I expect you to take this seriously."

This is my last chance to make a case for why I should be allowed to work with my friends. Video isn't my thing, I don't know this girl, and maybe I can show Mr. Valakis how much I can contribute to something I really do care about.

"But I really think I can add so much more if I—"

"Get to work, Chelsea," he says. "And don't ever laugh at someone like that again. In my class or anywhere else."

I walk back to my desk and try to grab my stuff and go to the front of the room without anybody noticing.

I can't believe this is happening. What happened to the silver lining?

I have to work on a project I don't care about at all. And on top of that, I have to work with Dina, this super-weird video girl. This is eighth grade; we're the oldest in the school. I've been looking forward to being in eighth grade since sixth grade, and it's supposed to be awesome. But it's starting to feel awful.

If only Kendall and Molly had kept me in the loop, I could be in the back of the room working with them right now.

Why didn't they keep me in the loop?

Do they know more about my secret than I think they know?

Suddenly, my worry about working with the new girl turns into worry about whether my friends know about everything that's happened.

I never had to worry about two things at once before, and I really don't like it.

I sit down next to Dina, low in my chair, thinking that if I sit like that, people won't notice what's actually happening here.

"It's good you're into video or whatever because this is so not my thing," I mumble.

"Oh," she says, still grinning, "It's really cool to capture stories on film. Or in this case, video. You can get really great stuff with just a simple video camera." It seems like she's waiting for me to say something, which I don't. So she just shrugs and keeps smiling at me. "I used to video something random every day at my old school. And then my friends and I would watch them over and over again."

I'm in hell. A brand-new kind of hell that I never knew about and didn't know existed before this very moment. All I can do is pray that one day things will be back to normal, the way they used to be, the way they're supposed to be. And I just hope beyond hope that Mr. Valakis doesn't make us work on this after school, at each other's houses.

I can't have that. For a million different reasons.

DINA

Video tip: The 180-degree rule: When shooting
a two-way interview with two cameras, keep both
on the same side of the action.

I'm snuggled in bed under my covers processing my
first day at Rockwood Hills Middle School. What amazes me
most is how the smallest little actions can have an impact on
the rest of your life.

If I hadn't had my camera out, if I hadn't been playing
with it because I felt uncomfortable that no one, not one
single person, was talking to me, then I wouldn't be making
this video—with Chelsea, of all people.

Chelsea, the girl who thinks she owns the school. And
maybe she does. Only time will tell. Chelsea's the girl that
every girl wants to be like, and if they can't be like her, they
want to be best friends with her. Even if they don't admit it.

I figured her out in about ten seconds.

It was easy—I used to be that girl. And I'll be that girl again. Either that or I'll be that girl's friend, which is just as good.

My cell phone rings, and I don't even have to look at it to know who it is.

I don't have to say hello, either. She'll just start talking.

And she does. "So, what's it like? You've been there one day. Do you have a million friends already? Who'd you sit with at lunch?" It's Ali. She's bombarding me with questions, like always. Before I moved, we decided we'd talk or video-chat every night at eight thirty, after dinner and before the good shows.

"It's okay." I'm not sure what to tell her. She's my best friend, and I usually tell her everything. But I can't be honest with her. Not yet, anyway. I can't tell her how I didn't really have anyone to sit with at lunch so I sat at the end of this one table, toward the back. It was a table full of girls who didn't really seem to go together, like mismatched socks. They were stuck together because they had nowhere else to be. I can't tell her about the whole potato chip thing. "I mean, really, it was just my first day. I didn't know what to expect."

"Yes, you did." Ali sighs. "We thought you'd be, like, I don't know, something, someone cool right away. We thought it'd be a utopia, the way your mom described it."

Ali's right about my mom. She talks about Long Island like it's paradise. *They even have drive-throughs where you can get milk and eggs and all the essentials.* She told us that a billion times. She lived here until she was a ten, so she has all these happy little-kid memories of it, like the town Memorial Day parades and ice cream trucks and stuff. And it's true that you're not likely to find drive-through places to get milk in rural Massachusetts.

"Yeah, well, maybe it is." I force myself to perk up. "I didn't say it was all bad. I'm still getting used to things."

"Yeah, that's true, Deenie." Ali pauses. "I miss you, though. Like today, at lunch, they had sloppy joes and I was singing that Adam Sandler song to myself and I wished so much that you were there to sing it with me."

"I know. I miss you, too, Al." I do miss her. She's the only other girl our age that even knows the sloppy joes song. And it isn't easy to move to a new school in eighth grade, but I have to make the best of it. I have to be happy here. My parents are beyond psyched to be here. My dad's a partner in this great firm. We live fifteen minutes from my grandparents. On paper, everything looks awesome.

Ali's still talking about her day. I'm trying to picture it. What would it be like if I was still there? Would we be in math together? Would I be at her house studying right now? Probably.

It's not like I've even been gone for that long. Just last week I was at my old school. But I have to admit, even then I didn't feel like I belonged. It was like I already had one foot out the door.

Our move was delayed because our new house wasn't ready yet. My parents and brother went to live with my grandparents for a few weeks, while I got to stay behind and live with Ali. I wanted to squeeze out the last few drops of Sheffield. And it was pretty awesome, like a sleepover every single night.

Ali and I fantasized about what life would be like on Long Island. I don't know why, but I pictured boys walking me home from school, kind of old-fashioned. And Ali said she thought there'd be a lot of dances. She thought it would feel like real middle school.

Our school—well, my old school—definitely didn't feel like real middle school. It was more like a tiny step up from elementary school. We didn't even change rooms for most classes, and we had to be called up to get our hot lunch. The whole grade ate together.

But the thing about my old school was that kids were just accepted, even if they were a little different from everyone else. Like Ramona Bevins, who said she enjoyed watching traffic, or Simon Tome, who had three pet snakes and brought them in on Fridays. At my old school, the lockers weren't even lockers; they were cubbies. No one stole anything. Not even once.

And no one was very mean.

No one crunched potato chips into someone else's bag.

I may have only been at Rockwood Hills for one day, but something tells me it's different. When I sat down at a table in the cafeteria, the kids sitting there barely even smiled. And in homeroom, Chelsea Stern and all those girls she's friends with were making a list of all the boys they thought were cute. When this other girl who wanted to sit down near them came over, they said, "This seat's taken. Sorry." But they weren't sorry.

And then there's Chelsea's whole attitude about working with me.

It's different here—very different. But I can't admit that to anyone. Not yet, anyway. I tell Ali more about my day, about the video and Chelsea and anything else I can think of, until I run out of ideas.

"Well, I gotta go," Ali says. "We have a huge sosh test tomorrow."

"We do?" I ask, not even realizing what I'm saying.

"Oh, sorry." She pauses. "I do."

Right then, it all hits me. Ali and I really don't go to school together anymore. We've been in school together since kindergarten, but I don't live in Massachusetts anymore. I live on Long Island.

And I don't have any friends.

"Bye, Al," I say.

"Bye, Dina. Can't wait to hear more about that girl you're working on the video with. Maybe you can text me a picture of you guys in matching shirts or something."

"Oh, shut up," I say. "You know you're the only one I match with."

"Yeah. For now."

Ali's jealous. She doesn't realize that she actually has absolutely nothing to be jealous about, but it'd take too long to explain that. So I don't. Instead, I imagine what it would be like if there was actually something for her to be jealous of. If Chelsea and I were actually friends.

My mom knocks on my door. She says she wants to hear all about my day.

"I told you guys over dinner," I say.

"I know." She smiles, like she's expecting more. "But girl stuff. Any cute boys in your grade? Any new friends? Give me the gossip."

She has this look on her face like she's expecting something really exciting. What, though? That I already have a boyfriend? That I already have a million friends?

"Actually, I didn't tell you about this project I'm working on," I start. "Do you know about the fiftieth-anniversary thingie?"

"Yeah, we got something about it in the mail." Her whole face perks up. "It seems like a really fun event. One of the moms I met at the PTA meeting said people are going all out—new dresses, getting their hair done, all that. I'm excited. It sounds fun, doesn't it?"

She's too excited about everything, too happy to be here, to ever tell her the truth about how I feel. "Yeah, definitely. So anyway, I had my video camera out, and then the teacher suggested I make some kind of 'day in the life' video for it."

"That's so great, sweetie!"

I kind of hate when my mom calls me sweetie; I'm not sure why. I sit back against the pillows on my bed. "This other girl in my social studies class is working on it with me."

"Really? Tell me about her."

"She's really popular."

"So? You're popular."

I glare at her. I don't need a mom pep talk right now. "I have homework to do."

"You okay, Dina?"

"I'm fine, Mom. Why?"

"Just checking."

My mom closes the door, and I start to think more about my day. Is it possible to already know that this school is so different from my old school? Do I just miss what I was used to, or is it really a bad place? How can I know for sure?

And how am I supposed to make a video about the school

when I just started and the girl I'm working with doesn't care about it at all?

Chelsea has everything going for her—pretty in a way that seems like she doesn't even try to look good, lots of friends, always someone to talk to.

She seemed so annoyed to have to work with me. She seemed weirded out when I said how much I liked shooting videos.

I stare at my bare walls, wishing that my dad had had a chance to hang up my pictures, when my cell phone vibrates.

> Don't be sad, Didi. Soon everyone will love u as much as I do. xo Al

She's right. I shouldn't be sad. Nothing good ever comes from feeling bad for yourself.

It was just my first day. First days of anything are always hard.

4

CHELSEA

Sasha Preston piece of advice: If people around you are grumpy, try to make them laugh. It may seem annoying at first, but it will work eventually.

I hate when I come home from school and my dad's still in his workout clothes. He works out, like, four hours a day now, like he's training for the Olympics or something. Most people would be impressed by this, but it makes me nervous. It seems like his day hasn't even started, even though it's almost time for dinner. I don't know if he or my mom cares, but everything about it upsets me because it's a sign that things aren't the way they're supposed to be. My dad's supposed to be wearing fancy pinstriped suits and ironed shirts and colorful ties, and he's supposed to come in just before dinner and take his shoes off and ask Alexa and me how our days were.

He's not supposed to be in workout clothes at dinnertime.

Every time I see him like that, I get even more worried. If this is how bad it is now, how much worse is it going to get? One day he stays in workout clothes and the next day he won't leave his room? I feel like that could totally happen.

My mom just pretends everything is fine, and I guess it could be worse. They could be fighting all the time. I'll take pretending over fighting any day.

"Chelsea," I hear my mom calling from downstairs. "Dinner."

My mom doesn't cook and doesn't feel bad about it, either, not a bit. But that's another thing that's changed around here—now she kind of pretends to cook. She'll pick up an already-cooked chicken and make a side dish, or sometimes she'll pick up a side dish, too.

No one complains, though, so I don't either. It's funny how when you don't have anything to complain about, you complain all the time, and when you actually do have stuff to complain about, you just keep quiet.

"So, any news, anyone?" My mom looks around the table, smiling.

I can't tell them how I basically got in trouble and then was forced into working on this dumb video. I can't tell them because they'll be mad and disappointed in me, and it will make them more depressed than they already are. I want to do the best that I can with everything so they don't have anything extra to worry about.

I'm grateful Alexa speaks and I don't have to. "I got a ninety-seven on my spelling test," she says. She's in fourth grade, and she doesn't know how easy she has it.

"What happened to the other three points?" my dad asks. That's his thing; he always asks that. I could get a ninety-nine point nine and he'd still ask, "Where's the point one percent?" but he doesn't say it in a mean way. It's just that he finds it funny, and we find it funny, too.

I laugh. Now more than ever, my dad needs to know I still think he's funny.

"Daaaaad," Alexa groans. "It was the highest grade in my class."

"And Chels, how was your first day back?" my mom asks me.

"Fine." I eat a bite of chicken. Maybe they'll leave me alone if they see me eating.

"I bet everyone was psyched to see you," my dad says. "Did they roll out the red carpet?"

I laugh again.

"Myrna told me that Molly and Kendall are working on some kind of science experiment thing for the fiftieth anniversary. I didn't realize they were really into science. But I assume you're doing that, too?"

"No." I move my chicken around on my plate. "I missed the first month of school. Remember?"

"Chelsea," my dad warns. "Lose the attitude."

"Fine. Sorry." I roll my eyes. "I have homework to finish. May I be excused?"

My parents nod reluctantly, and I go up to my room. I can't believe I just lied to them that I have homework to finish and they bought it. Since when am I the kind of girl who lies to her parents? Since today, I guess. I also tried to lie to Mr. Valakis about the project, but that didn't work as well as lying to my parents.

I just hate when my mom hears things from Myrna or Gwen and then she talks to me all nonchalantly about it, when what she's really asking is if I'm doing what the other girls are doing. And if I'm not, why not?

I used to think it was great having friends who had moms who were friends with my mom. Like when we needed to go bra shopping, we all did it together, so it wasn't awkward. That kind of stuff.

But now it just feels like a competition that I'm always on the verge of losing, and the losing isn't even the worst part. It's the sadness in my mom's eyes when she realizes I'm losing.

I can't take it.

So I call Molly.

"How come you guys didn't save me a spot in what you're doing for the fiftieth-anniversary thing?" I ask without saying hello first. We're past the point of hello.

"What are you talking about?" she asks back. My nickname for Molly when we were four years old in nursery school was Mean Molly. She used to take the Velcro from her sneakers and scratch it on people's legs, and once she told our first-grade teacher she was fat, right to her face.

She's just mean; I've always thought so, but I stay friends with her anyway. Because the thing is, she's never been mean to me, just other people, and I guess I've always been afraid of what would happen if we stopped being friends. Then she'd be mean to me, obviously, and I couldn't handle that. I'd never admit that to anyone, but it's true.

"You, Kendall, and even Brie—who we're so not friends with—you're all working on the science fair stuff." I pause, waiting for her to say something. She doesn't. "I was out of school, so I didn't have a chance to sign up. And now I'm stuck doing this stupid video thing with that new girl."

"You mean that girl Dina?"

"Yeah. What other new girl is there?"

"She's weird. I can tell already. Did you see how she was, like, staring out the window the entire math period? She didn't take one note. And why does she even have a video camera with her? So weird."

I don't respond to that because I didn't call Molly to gossip about Dina. "Seriously, Molls. Why didn't you tell me about the project?"

"No offense, Chels." She pauses. She always starts sentences "no offense," especially when she's about to say something offensive. "But you're not really into science."

I snort. "And you are?"

"Well, yeah, kind of. Ever since my parents had that meeting with Mrs. Nodenski and they got me into honors." Through the phone I can hear her popping her gum. "And it's not like we're doing *science* science, like test tubes and beakers and microscopes. We're doing this study on how weather affects people's actions and moods—like, if they go shopping as much when it's raining as they do when it's sunny, stuff like that. We're spending a lot of time at the mall, taking surveys and counting people."

"Oh."

Molly huffs into the receiver. "Anyway, I'm sorry. We didn't mean to leave you out or anything on purpose. We just didn't think of it."

I sigh. That's almost worse. "I gotta go. See you tomorrow."

"You mad?" she whines. Molly has the worst whine in the world.

"A little. Mainly just annoyed." As soon as I say it, I want to take it back. I wasn't thinking, saying something like that. I wasn't thinking at all.

"Annoyed about what? We decorated your locker to welcome you back. And we have plans to go to the Cheesecake Factory Saturday night. Some of the guys might even be coming. You can totally sleep over after. And we can get a mani on Sunday. What's there to be annoyed about? Your life is totally great. Who cares about the fiftieth anniversary anyway? I mean, you—"

"Okay, you're right." I stop her. I can't listen to her babble on anymore. Even her trying to be nice has hints of meanness to it.

"Good. Glad you agree. See you tomorrow."

It's true that Molly doesn't really know all I have to be annoyed about, like our take-out rotisserie chicken instead of dinner out at Café Spuntino.

It's my fault she doesn't know, because I haven't told her, and I don't plan to.

I wish that if I told her and Kendall, everything would stay the same between us. But that's just not how it is with us, and I've lived here long enough to know that.

I flop back onto my bed, open my backpack, and look at my planner to see what homework I have to do.

I don't have too much. I think the teachers are being nice and helping me ease back into school, plus I kept up with some of the work while I was home.

The handout about the fiftieth-anniversary projects from Mr. Valakis falls out of my planner, and I'm forced to face the fact that I actually have to do this. And it's not going to be done in one day, either.

Maybe I could scheme my way out of this by having my mom and dad go in and talk to Mr. Oliver, the principal, and say that I'm really better suited for another kind of project. Parents around here always get their kids out of stuff; it wouldn't be hard.

But then that would mean my parents would have to go into school, and maybe they'd run into someone they knew and then soon enough everyone would know everything.

And besides, I don't really want to fight to work with Kendall and Molly. I want them to fight to work with me. But I don't think that's going to happen.

5

DINA

Video tip: If you need to make a cut in an interview,
use B-roll footage to cover it. Avoid jump cuts.

Day two is so much harder than day one. On day one it's
okay and acceptable to be a little frazzled and out of it. But
day two you're expected to know what's going on. You don't
have the excuse anymore. You can't just say, "Oh, it's my first
day," because it's not. And it's lame to go around saying, "Oh,
it's my second day." By the second day, no one cares. You still
feel new, and you still *are* new, but no one wants to help you
find your way.

Right now I'm in homeroom. I'm in the same exact seat
I sat in yesterday. All the rest of the kids are in different seats.
Some of them aren't even sitting down, or they're sitting on
the tops of the desks chatting with one another. And I'm just
sitting quietly staring at my planner because I don't really

know anyone well enough to chat with. And I don't want to do that whole introducing myself thing because, again, it's the second day, not the first.

Besides, I tried to be chatty in homeroom yesterday. It didn't get me anywhere.

Mrs. Welsh comes in. She takes our attendance and then goes on for ten minutes about the fiftieth anniversary and how we need to take our projects seriously.

I am taking it seriously. Even though I only learned about it yesterday.

"What are you doing for the project?" I ask the girl sitting next to me. It's the only thing I can think to say. She's wearing all black and trying to hide the fact that she's playing Tetris on her cell phone.

"I said I'd help with cleanup."

"You're allowed to do that?"

"No. But I'm already the poorest kid in the school so I might as well be treated like everyone else's housekeeper."

I gasp. Now I really can't think of anything to say.

She smiles. "I'm kidding. I just wanted to see how you'd react."

"Oh." I force a smile.

"I'm on Brainbusters."

"What's that?"

"The trivia team." She sits back in her chair and puts one foot up on the side of the desk. "I'm Lee, by the way."

"Dina." I feel like we should shake hands or something. Who is Lee friends with? Definitely not Chelsea Stern and those girls. And I don't think she and I have much in common, either.

"I know. I saw you yesterday." The bell rings finally and Lee grabs her backpack with patches halfheartedly sewn on. "Good luck working with Chelsea Stern, by the way. I feel for you." She looks down at my bag. "Oh, um, sorry about that."

It happened again. I was chipped. If it keeps happening, I'm just going to start eating the crumbs. They're too delicious to waste.

Lee walks on ahead of me. I try to figure out exactly what she means about Chelsea. I'm not sure if I really even want to know.

Soon it's social studies again, which means video time.

I get to Mr. Valakis's classroom and take a seat in the middle and wait for class to start. So far there's no sight of Chelsea.

"If you're here early, you can get started," Mr. Valakis says. He has a much more laid-back tone today, and he's sitting on the desk. He's wearing those ultrathick wool socks people wear for hiking in the middle of the winter, even though it's really not that cold.

So everyone gets started working, and I just sit here

writing down different ideas for the video: a photo montage with voice-over, a skit about Rockwood Hills Middle School, maybe something totally different altogether like a video about the ways kids around here are giving back to their community? There are so many possibilities.

"Dina?" Mr. Valakis asks.

I look up.

"Are you getting started? Not to put pressure on you, but you and Chelsea are already behind, you know. The event is in a little less than two months."

"Yeah, I'm writing down all the ideas I have." I smile, but for some reason he doesn't respond. "I have my camera and everything."

"Okeydokey."

Finally, Chelsea and her friends stroll in. They're carrying Dunkin' Donuts cups. And I thought I was the only eighth grader who drank coffee. I got the habit from my bubbie and her friends. They always sit around sipping coffee and eating babka and telling jokes, and I join them whenever I can. It's a grandmas-telling-jokes club, and even though I'm nowhere near grandma age, I really enjoy it. I've been doing it since I was really little, like six or seven, which is how I developed a love for coffee. I don't believe that whole it'll-stunt-your-growth thing.

"You're late," Mr. Valakis says to them.

"We were in Mr. Oliver's office," one of Chelsea's friends says, talking with her back to Mr. Valakis as she walks to her seat.

"With coffee?"

"Uh-huh," another friend says. "We were discussing the anniversary gala. Our moms were there, too, and they brought coffee for everyone."

Mr. Valakis squints a little like he doesn't quite believe them. "I see."

Chelsea and her friends keep sipping their coffee as they start to work on their project. I expect Chelsea to come over to me to get to work on ours. But she doesn't. She stays with them.

I just sit here. I want to go over to them. I want to tell Chelsea my ideas, but I feel like I can't.

The clock on the wall with the oversized numbers ticks loudly, and I stare at it, noticing minute after minute go by. We literally haven't done a single thing on this project. It's only my second day here and I'm already a delinquent. Everyone around me is working.

This isn't me. I'm not that girl, the one who didn't do what she was supposed to do.

I stare at my notebook and keep writing stuff. That way

if anyone asks, I can just say I'm jotting down ideas for the project. Which I am. Trying to, at least.

"Chelsea," Mr. Valakis calls out to her. "Please get to work. I don't want to have to say it again."

She huffs like someone offended her and stands up. Her friends say things like "Good luck, Chels" and "Bye, Chelsers, have fun" in these totally sarcastic, mocking tones.

After Chelsea sits down next to me, she starts talking. "So we just had this meeting with Mr. Oliver. He's our principal—you know that, right? Anyway, my friends convinced me to see if I could get switched onto the science projects group with them, but apparently he feels really strongly about this video thing and he thinks I can do a good job with it." She rolls her eyes.

"Yeah, well, obviously I need your help learning about the school." I hear her friends in the back of the room talking and laughing. I try to ignore them. "But I can handle the video stuff."

She stands up, puts her hands on her hips, and yells to her friends to be quiet. Then she sits back down.

"Well, we'll just get it done as quickly as we can." She takes the last sip of coffee. "But we're gonna have to meet after school in the library to do the shooting. We can't disrupt any classes during the school day."

"Oh." I try to stop myself from jumping up and down in my seat. Chelsea and me, hanging out after school! This is great. And I didn't have to say it first! This is my chance to have friends the way I thought I would. My chance to be someone here. My chance to be happy here.

"Yeah, I know." She rolls her eyes again. She thinks I'm upset. Wow—I didn't realize I was that hard to read. "Anyway, meet me in the library after ninth period. We'll see what we can do."

I nod. The bell rings, and everyone leaves the classroom.

I walk out alone, but I don't dwell on it. I feel hopeful. I feel like things are looking up.

CHELSEA

Sasha Preston piece of advice: Compliment
someone at least once a day. It makes everyone happy.

"They're hot, right?" Molly asks. We're in the cafeteria finishing lunch and she's standing up with her back to us and her
head turned over her shoulder, like a wannabe supermodel.
"Three hundred. But they only made, like, fifty pairs, so they're
kind of like a collectible."

"Yeah, I'm on the waiting list at Denim Spectator. They're
trying to see if they can find me a pair. They've even called the
manufacturer," Kendall adds.

The thing with Kendall is that she always has to have
exactly what everyone else has. It started when she and I had
the same baby fur coat in playgroup when we were two years
old, and it's been that way ever since. Usually, I'm the one she
tries to clone, but she's been acting more like Molly lately.

I wonder if it's because she's noticed that I don't have the newest, coolest stuff before everyone else does anymore.

I should have those jeans. I'm the one who got everyone into the brand in the first place after I went to the trunk show with my dad and one of his colleagues. I hate that I get into a bad mood just because I don't have those jeans, and won't ever have those jeans.

"Are you getting them, Chels?" Kendall asks.

"Yeah, of course." I smile. "I just haven't been shopping so much because of the mono."

"Well, if Denim Spectator finds me a pair, I'll just pick them up for you and you can pay me back," she says. "No problem."

I nod and swallow hard. I pray they don't find them. It's weird Kendall cares about me having them. Usually, she's only concerned that she has what everyone else has.

"Sucks you have to hang out with that girl after school," Kendall says. "I'm so sorry we didn't get you into our science group. I totally thought buttering up Mr. Oliver with Dunkin' Donuts would work."

I guess I made them feel guilty, so they did end up fighting to work with me—for a few minutes, at least—so that was good.

"Yeah, I have to meet up with the new girl. How else am I gonna finish the stupid video?" I eat the last section of my clementine. "I shouldn't have laughed in front of Mr. Valakis. Apparently, he doesn't have a sense of humor."

They both shrug. "That girl is strange," Molly says. "The way she videos random stuff. She doesn't even have any friends here, so what's she videoing?" Molly stares at Dina as she talks about her. Molly doesn't even try to be slick when she's talking about people. It's like she wants them to know she's talking about them.

"I have no idea." I look over at Dina. She's sitting only one table away from us, and I wonder if she can hear what we're saying. I hope not; that would make the whole working together thing even more awkward.

She's sitting with the studying-obsessed girls who wanted to start a field hockey team last year. They never seem to really like each other, either. They sit quietly at lunch with books on their laps, studying and barely talking to each other. Dina has her camera out of course, and she's just randomly taping the cafeteria. Who does that?

We're all watching her, and then we see Ross walk over to her.

"Guys, Ross Grunner is walking over to that girl right now," Molly says, as if we can't all see it ourselves.

He kneels down next to Dina's seat and whispers something to her. She looks all confused, then she smiles and says something back, and then he gets up and walks away.

I can't look, and yet all I want to do is look. I keep looking away and then turning to look again. It could have been a bad clementine, but my stomach is doing flips right now.

"Aren't you going to stop that, Chels?" Kendall asks. "Ross is talking to the new girl more than he's talking to you."

I don't say anything. It's not really that big of a deal, but the way they're reacting is stressing me out. I'm ripping my clementine peel into a million little pieces.

"We should make a video of her!" Kendall yelps. "And, like, show it to people and stuff. Wouldn't that be hilarious?"

"Do you know how to even use a camera, Ken?" Molly elbows Kendall. "Come on."

"Yeah, there's one on my phone!"

Finally, the bell rings and we all leave the cafeteria. I block out the fact that Ross was just talking to Dina and I have absolutely no idea why. I block out the fact that it seems like Kendall wants to torment the new girl.

Have they really stooped that low? Have *I* stooped that low, too?

After school, I meet Dina in the library. She's sitting at one of the back tables, writing in a Curious George notebook. It's one of those thick, sturdy ones, with a red binding and a bright yellow cover, and I immediately want it. I have a soft spot for school supplies. I'm staring at it so I almost trip on one of the blue library carts that's sitting in the middle of the floor.

"Oh, sorry," this kid says, running over to move it.

"Don't worry about it," I say. I can't think of his name. He was new last year, but he hasn't been in any of my classes. I think something happened to him over the summer—he's turned cute out of nowhere. He has ultrashort brown hair and very blue eyes. You don't see that combination very often.

As I get closer to Dina, I notice how neat her handwriting is and spot the pretty turquoise ring on her middle finger.

There are cool things about her when you take the time to pay attention. Maybe Ross realized that.

"Hey," I say. I want to compliment her on her notebook and her ring, but I don't. The words don't come out.

"Oh, hi!" Dina's way too cheery for three fifteen, and it bugs me when people are too cheery for no reason at all. I want to tell her to cheer down. "I was just jotting down notes. I have a million ideas, but here's the best one: I can tape and you can be the star of the video! Like how Mr. Valakis said 'a day in the life' of a student here. Well, this can be a day in your life!"

"Um." At first, I think that sounds like an amazing idea. Who doesn't want to be a star? It could be like my own reality show, a camera following me around. Then I could be discovered and become the next Sasha Preston. But after I think about it for a few minutes, I change my mind. "That would be cool, but I don't think so."

"Why not?" she asks. "You know everyone at school, you've lived here awhile, you're perfect for 'a day in the life of a Rockwood Hills student.' I'll do all the shooting and editing and putting it all together. You'd just have to be you!"

"I said no." Dina doesn't even know me. How does she know I'd be a good star for the video? I can't look at her, so I look at my phone instead. Kendall sent a text about how they're all going to Ross's house to order in sushi and play video games and I should meet up with them. I don't want to be here, but I'm not sure I want to be there, either. I'm sure everyone is already talking about their plans for winter break and if they're flying first-class. And I'm a little sick of Kendall and Molly trying to convince me that I like Ross. I'm not sure I do. "Okay?"

"Okay," Dina says under her breath, like she knows she's been defeated, and she stays quiet for a few minutes.

"It just wouldn't be good to focus on one person in the video," I say as an excuse because I feel bad but also because I can't stand the awkward silence anymore. "I know it's a day in the life, but we should focus on more than one person."

There. That's a good explanation, if I do say so myself, and I bet she'll be into that idea because she probably wants to meet people around here. Yeah, she's only been here two days, but she barely talks to anyone, not even to the girls she eats lunch with.

"Oh!" she yells suddenly. "I have an idea! I can just get random shots of the school and kids in the hallways and we can put upbeat, fun music over it, and it can show all kids in their natural school environment. It'll be all B-roll."

"B-roll?" Right when I start to feel bad about being rude to her, she gets way too excited about something and starts using weird video terms and I feel myself getting annoyed with her all over again.

"Yeah, it means, like, background shots, shots of the surroundings, and people walking around and stuff. But I think it would be neat for this," she says.

I text Kendall that I'm stuck at school working on the video and can't come to Ross's house, but that she has to tell me everything that happens as soon as she's home. "That could be okay, I guess."

Dina huffs. I guess she senses my lack of enthusiasm. "Well, you've lived here a long time, haven't you? Don't you have any ideas?"

My phone vibrates again, a text from Molly this time.

ur lame. ☺ jk. But we miss u! ross is gonna forget he likes you. we never see u anymore.

"Um." I crack my knuckles, praying something will come to me. Molly thinks I'm lame, and she knows something's up, but she hasn't figured out what it is yet. Even though I'm not sure I like Ross, it still feels good to know he likes me, or at least that's what Kendall thinks. I wonder if he told them anything about what he said to Dina at lunch. "Nope. No ideas."

Dina sighs, and twirls a pen around her fingers like a miniature baton. "Well, we should do a good job, right? Aren't there going to be a ton of people there? Like, the whole school and parents and everyone?"

I nod. "Yeah, I think so."

"So think about my idea of background footage and candid shots," she says. "The parents will be excited to see glimpses of their kids' lives at school, and the kids will be excited to see their friends."

She's trying so hard to convince me, but I just don't really care that much. I want to get it done as quickly as possible. Lately, all I want to do is get through things and have them be over with so I can move on to the next thing.

It can be kind of nice to have someone try really hard to get you to agree, or try really hard to get you to like them.

Sometimes it's really pathetic, but other times it's pretty flattering.

Right now it's one of the flattering times.

"Okay . . ." I smile slowly. "Let's do it."

The thing about this Dina girl is that you want to hate her but something about her makes you not totally hate her. There's a shred of likeability in her. And she doesn't even feel weird about being new. It's like she's from some alternate universe where people don't worry about what others think of them. I'm not going to lie—I'm a little jealous. I want to go to that universe sometimes. A lot of times, actually. Especially now.

"I know how we can get started." She caps her pen and closes her Curious George notebook. "Ready?"

I nod.

"Let's look at yearbooks. Since you know everyone here, you can tell me about them, and maybe there are some people better than others to sort of focus on. Maybe I can even pan the yearbooks in the shots. That'd be so cool-looking, and it would help highlight the history of the school! It'll help show the transformation from the school of the past to the school today. And who doesn't like looking at yearbooks?" She jumps up. "It'll be fun!"

"Okay . . ."

"And if we look at really old yearbooks, it'll be fun to see people's crazy hair. People always had the weirdest hairstyles back in the day. Didn't they?"

"Totally. But I don't know how far back the yearbooks go. I'll go find Mr. Singer." I wonder if I'll see that kid again, and if I do, I hope I remember his name.

"Who?"

"Oh, the librarian. He's actually kind of cool."

When I get back from looking for Mr. Singer, I realize what I've done—something totally careless and stupid. Like an absolute total idiot, I left my cell phone on the table, just sitting there, not even with the keypad locked. The screen on my BlackBerry is bright, and on it there's another text from Molly.

> can't believe ur missing this. having fun with weird video girl?

Dina looks at the phone and then up at me and back at the phone again.

Things just went from bad to worse. Why did she have to see that?

Yeah, I don't want to be working with her, but I'm not like Molly, someone who's totally fine with insulting other people. But in all fairness, even Molly didn't expect that Dina would see it.

I'm the moron who let that happen.

"Sorry," I mumble. "It's just Molly. She doesn't realize what she says half the time."

"I get that you guys don't know me, and I'm new and that automatically makes me uncool, even though I sort of thought that would make me stand out kind of in a cool way," Dina says all in a rush, "but what I don't get is why you're all so weirded out with the video thing. You have a video camera on your BlackBerry right there, the one that just vibrated and insulted me."

She's pointing at my phone, and I cover my mouth because I'm about to crack up. Dina's actually kind of funny sometimes. "It's just—I don't know—unusual, I guess."

She nods like she's trying to understand what I'm saying. She doesn't say anything for a few seconds, and then she asks, "Did you find the librarian or the yearbooks? I have to go soon, and we've accomplished nothing."

"I'm sorry you saw that, okay?" I say again because I don't know what else to do. And then I hear Mr. Singer's unmistakable whistling. "I'll make it up to you, I swear. Right now, actually. I'll get the yearbooks."

I head over to the circulation desk, but before I can ask Mr. Singer for anything, Dina yells from across the library.

"I actually have to go," she says. "My mom forgot my

brother has a dentist appointment, so she needs to pick me up now. I'll meet you here after school tomorrow."

At least she says she'll meet me here tomorrow. That's kind of a good thing because now that I think about it, talking about the project for a few minutes was actually kind of fun. It was a little chunk of time when I wasn't thinking about things at home or worrying about my friends finding out about everything.

And I got to see that cute kid with the libary cart.

Dina doesn't wait for me to say anything back, she just leaves, her oversized mom-looking tote bag slung over her right shoulder. That's what I get for offering to make it up to her, even though I didn't really say the mean thing—Molly did.

Maybe I should text Molly and tell her she shouldn't have said that, but the truth is, the only reason I'm mad is because Dina saw it. If she hadn't seen it, it wouldn't have even fazed me.

But that's how I feel about everything lately—once it's out in the open, it's much, much worse.

7

DINA

Video tip: Use the eyes to draw emotion.
Cut on the blinks.

Even after a few days, that text message lingers in my brain. Why did I have to see it? It's not like I couldn't guess what they were saying. But seeing it makes it a million times worse. I couldn't even tell Ali about it. And forget about telling my mom—that would crush her. It would be like I told her I was I moving to the moon or converting to another religion or something.

But seeing that text message struck something in me. My situation is dire. I need to make Chelsea realize I'm cool. I know that if I were truly cool, I wouldn't care about making her and her friends realize it. But oh, well. I guess I'm only moderately cool. But moderately cool is still something.

We're in the library after school, Chelsea's sitting at the

table texting and I'm reading an article online from the *Berkshire Eagle*. It may be weird that I still read the newspaper from where I used to live, but I like to keep up to date about what's going on there. The big Berkshire arts festival is this weekend and all these famous photographers and musicians are coming. There will be food vendors, too, selling fancy croissants and exotic cheeses and this amazing butternut squash soup. It's painful to even think about it—this is the first arts festival I'm missing.

Mr. Singer brings a huge stack of yearbooks over to the table, and I close the library laptop and return it to him. The yearbooks smell old, but it's that good old smell, antique and special and delicate.

"I've spent the past few days looking for other yearbooks for you girls, but I'm sorry to say we don't have yearbooks going back all fifty years," Mr. Singer tells us. "I think some got lost in the renovation."

"Oh." That seems sad to me. How can you lose a yearbook? It's like a piece of history. I bet the Smithsonian never loses anything. "Isn't there, like, a school archivist or something?"

Mr. Singer sighs. "Not that I know of. Anyway, this should be a good start."

"It's so sad that all the yearbooks aren't here," I say out loud and then feel kind of pathetic that this upsets me. Since it's only my first week at the school, I'm really not sure why I care so much. Getting sad about old yearbooks isn't going to help convince Chelsea of my coolness.

"You're probably the only one who cares this much about yearbooks," Chelsea says flatly.

See what I mean?

"Well, I guess we should put them in order by year, and then we can get a better idea of the history."

"I'm so tired," Chelsea says, putting her feet up on one of the library chairs and then looking around like she's scared someone is going to catch her doing it. "Maybe we can start working on the project fully on Monday. I mean, it is Friday afternoon. All my friends are at the mall right now."

"Oh, yeah." My first Friday without Ali plans. Without ice cream at Bev's and Baba Louie's pizza for dinner and a sleepover.

It feels too sad to think about. "I forgot it was Friday when I agreed to meet with you," Chelsea says, looking at her phone like she's waiting for a text or a call.

"Well, my mom's picking me up at five, so I might as well stay here," I say.

"Can't you just call her on her cell?"

I shrug. "I could, but there's really no rush for me to get home. All I'll find there is more unpacking to do. Kind of depressing."

Chelsea leans her elbow on the table and then rests her chin in her palm. "Yeah, well, I don't really have anywhere to go, either."

"You just said all your friends were at the mall."

"Yeah, but there's no point in going now."

Chelsea may be the most popular girl at Rockwood Hills Middle School, but she's kind of nuts. I don't know how to read her. One minute she's all gung ho and the next minute she's not interested at all. And then she switches again.

She opens the yearbook on the top of the pile. It's from only a couple years ago. She starts flipping through the pages haphazardly, responding to texts every three seconds. You'd think she would lie low on the text messaging after the debacle from the other day. Apparently not.

I'm looking at the pages over her shoulder when I spot her. "Oh my God." I can't believe what I'm seeing.

"What?" Chelsea asks.

"Did you just see who was on that page?"

Chelsea turns back a page and squints. "Um . . . Mrs. Matrizzi, the computer science teacher who looks like a real-life version of the mom from *The Family Guy*?"

"Oh, well, yeah." I laugh about that for a second, then point to what I saw. "But no, look at her. That's Sasha Preston. Like *the* Sasha Preston, from *Sasha Says So*. She went here? Oh my God. Did you know that? That's so, so, so coo—"

Chelsea rolls her eyes for the billionth time. At least that's how it feels. "Are you serious? You didn't know that?"

I'm tempted to lie, because admitting I didn't know Sasha Preston went here will probably decrease my coolness level even further. But I'm a bad liar. "Nope. Had no idea."

"Yeah, she graduated from here four years ago. She left here, got discovered, and then her show started. She has private tutors now and doesn't go to high school."

We're still looking at her picture in the yearbook. She looks pretty similar to how she looks in the show—except her hair is a little longer and not really styled at all in the picture. She looks normal, average, like any girl you'd see at any school in the country. I wonder if anyone could have predicted that she'd become a star.

It's hard to imagine her having to play badminton and having to stand on the hot-food lunch line and having to change in the gym locker room. Did she get chipped?

Sasha Says So is about this girl who runs an advice column in the school paper that gets to be so popular she sets up a booth where people can come and ask for advice. It's cheesy but funny at the same time. It's the kind of show you like more the more you watch it, so it's better in reruns. But it's really popular—it wins the Kids' Choice Award every year.

Looking at her picture in the yearbook makes me wonder

what her real life is like. Or *was* like when she went here. Did she like the school? Was she popular? Was she a Chelsea? Or a *me?*

Chelsea and I keep flipping through the old yearbook. We're looking at everything but mostly looking for pictures of Sasha Preston. We find her in the index, and she has at least twenty page numbers after her name. Most people only have two or three.

"I can't believe you never looked for pictures of her in the yearbooks before," I say.

Chelsea shrugs.

"Oh my God, this is it!" I scream.

"What?" Chelsea says as she puts her hair up in a ponytail. Her phone keeps vibrating, but she ignores it.

"What we'll do for the video! A day in the life of a Rockwood Hills student? Well, hello! Here's one! And a famous one." I take a deep breath. Finally, a good idea is coming to me. "Even if she's not the whole video, we can put Sasha in it somewhere!"

Chelsea shakes her head, not even looking at me. She finally picks up her phone so it stops vibrating. I can tell from where I'm sitting that she has three missed calls. "Are you kidding?" I can't tell if she's talking to me or to her phone. "You don't get it. She doesn't live here anymore. She's, like, famous. I know you came from Massachusetts, and you don't know that much about pop culture, but she's not just going to be in our video."

Okay. Did she really need to insult where I'm from?

"First of all," I say, "I'm from the Berkshires. It's like the cultural capital of the world. Okay, at least the state. But that's not even the point." I stop talking and wait for her to look up from her phone. She finally does. "I know Sasha doesn't live here. But that doesn't mean we can't find her."

Chelsea closes the yearbook and pushes her chair back from the table. "Look, my parents know everyone around here, and they don't know Sasha and they don't know her parents, so there's no way we're going to just find her." She leans down and grabs a bottle of Vitaminwater from her bag. After an extra-long sip she says, "So can you just stop being weird and tell me what we have to do to make a decent video for this thing?"

"Well, you have to care about it just the littlest bit," I say. "Can you at least do that? I don't know what's so hard in your life that you can't just do your part on this project."

I don't know why I said that. My whole plan was getting Chelsea to like me, and getting her friends to realize I'm cool and like me, too. Criticizing people never really gets them to like you. That's one thing I know.

Chelsea starts sniffling. It seems like she might cry. Making someone cry *definitely* isn't a way to get them to like you.

She's going to cry. I know it. Then I won't just be weird. I'll be mean, too.

"Fine, I'll try," she says at last. She doesn't cry. At least that's something. "I'll take the recent yearbooks and I'll put Post-it notes on the pictures of kids we should try to get in the video." She huffs and then starts making a pile of the yearbooks. "Is that good enough?"

"Fine." I open the next yearbook in the pile, the one from last year. "So who would be good on this page?" I start at the beginning of the alphabet.

"Um . . ." Chelsea scans the page. "I don't know any of those people."

"Haven't you been going here since kindergarten?"

She nods.

"You don't know anyone in our grade?" I ask.

"Okay, I know who they *are,* obviously, but I don't talk to them." She huffs again. "Let's just go to the next page."

We get to the next page, and the only people she picks out are her friend Kendall and this boy Ross, who I actually know because he randomly came up and talked to me the other day in the cafeteria. He's pretty much the only person I know here, besides Chelsea.

"You're picking your friends," I say. "We can't just do a video of your friends."

"I can't work with you!" she says, and throws down the yearbook. "You're insane. You're more insane than I thought at first."

"Really?" I ask. I'm not offended, just genuinely curious. What did I do that was so crazy?

"Really." She picks up her bag and makes a pile of the yearbooks.

"Girls, if you're using the yearbooks for the project, feel free to take them home," Mr. Singer tells us from the circulation desk, interrupting our conversation.

"Thank you so much!" I say, and then realize I probably shouldn't be this excited about taking a bunch of dusty old yearbooks home.

Chelsea takes a few yearbooks and puts them in her bag. She raises her eyebrows like she also thinks it's cool that we can take them home.

I want to get back to our conversation. "Well, what would you say if I told you I could find Sasha Preston? And I could get her to talk to us?"

"You can't find her. I just told you that. So I'd say the same thing—you're insane." She picks up her bag and walks out of the library, reading something on her phone instead of looking ahead. Then she stops and looks back at me. "But, fine, find her if you can. What do we have to lose? Just more time when we could be working on this dumb thing."

I nod.

"Tell me when you find her," she yells back to me as she's leaving the library. "I'll be holding my breath."

I smile even though she can't see me anymore.

After finding Sasha in that yearbook, and taking a few yearbooks home, I think I can consider today a success. Now all I have to do is convince Chelsea of the same thing.

8

CHELSEA

Sasha Preston piece of advice: Take a second to think before answering a question. It will prevent you saying something you may regret.

I'm going to the movies in a few hours, and my dad is still sleeping. It's after ten a.m. I hate when he does this. This is bad. This is a sign that he's really depressed and things have gotten worse and nobody is telling me what's going on. I can't tell if I want to know or if I don't want to know. When things reach a really bad point, they won't want to tell me; they'll feel like they need to protect me like I'm some little kid.

My mom is at the orthodontist with Alexa, and I'm dreading what happens when she comes home. And isn't fourth grade, like, really early to need braces? Why does Alexa have to have such bad teeth?

Braces are so expensive, and I know my mom's going to

show the bill to my dad and he's going to get weird. He'll try to act like he has everything under control, but I'll know the truth. I can always tell what's happening, even if people aren't saying it.

I hope Kendall's mom picks me up before they get home. But then I feel bad leaving Alexa to deal with the chaos all alone. She's only nine, after all.

As I'm waiting for Kendall's mom to arrive, I look at one of the yearbooks a little more closely.

When Mr. Singer told us we could take home the year-books, Dina was really excited about it. Like, crazy excited—like when Molly got the jeans excited.

She asked me what I was doing this weekend, and I swear she had this look in her eyes, like she wanted me to invite her to do something. She didn't say anything, though. It was just a feeling I got.

But there was no way in the world I was inviting her to hang out. For one thing, Molly and Kendall already think she's weird, and after that whole accidentally read text-message thing, I doubt they'd all get along. It was never going to happen.

The thing about my friends is that we were all paired up at birth to be friends. Before birth, really. Our moms all traveled in the same circle after college and then all moved to Rockwood Hills after living in Manhattan during their single and newly married days.

Sometimes I feel like the only reason I'm the way I am is because of my parents. But I guess that's true for everyone in some way.

The yearbook I'm looking at now is from 2006, from when Sasha Preston was in seventh grade.

That year, all the students got a little section to write messages to their friends and they were printed along with candid photos.

Hers says:

To Lulu and Fi, thanks for being the bestest of the best. Never forget midnight swims, taco charlies, and the red racer scooter. Next year, 8th grade! It will be totally radically amazing. Love and tacos, ha ha. xo Sash

It's so funny to read other people's private jokes. What in the world is taco charlies? And why didn't she put an apostrophe? It sounds like she has like an obsession with tacos. And the red racer scooter? Huh? It's probably pointless to wonder and try to figure this out.

In the yearbook last year, Molly, Kendall, and I wrote "BEEP BEEP BEEP" to each other because we were obsessed with the sound of Kendall's mom's car alarm. It was such a stupid thing, and no one else would ever get it or find it funny. But we found it totally hilarious. We were so immature.

Maybe there's something to that, something that would be good to add to the video. I mean, everyone has private jokes. Even the weirdos at school have private jokes with each other, right?

I can't believe I'm actually thinking about this video outside of school. What's happening to me? Is Dina's weirdness rubbing off on me?

I hear a honk and look outside to see Kendall's Range Rover in my driveway. I quickly shove the yearbook under one of the couch cushions, grab my jacket, and head outside.

Molly gives me a halfhearted smile as I get into the car.

"Hello, gorgeous," Kendall's mom says. "Did you cut your hair?"

"Nope." I shake my head.

"New shampoo?"

"I don't think so." I smile. "Guess it's just a good hair day." Kendall's mom is kind of obsessed with knowing every little detail about people, especially Kendall's friends and her friends. It's like she has an imaginary Excel spreadsheet in her brain that she's constantly updating.

"Well, you girls sure are heading out early today. I didn't

even know they showed movies this early," Kendall's mom says. "But I guess that's what happens when you're teenagers."

She's also kind of obsessed with the fact that we're teenagers.

Kendall turns around to look at us in the backseat and makes a face like her mom is a total imbecile. "Mom. I told you, we're not going to the movies until one. We're just meeting the guys at the mall before. Why are you so dense?"

"God. Sorry," Kendall's mom says. She doesn't even get mad when Kendall or her sisters talk to her like that. She cares so much that they like her that she'll basically let them do whatever they want.

"Is Grunner coming?" Molly asks me. "He didn't text Kendall back."

Kendall turns around and snorts.

"Yeah, he texted me this morning. He said he'd meet us by the smoothie place in the food court," I say. I push the window button down and open the window as far as it goes. It suddenly feels like a million degrees in here. I pull my hair up off the back of my neck to cool it.

"He texted you? Grunner texted you and you didn't even tell us?" Kendall's yelling, but her mom doesn't seem to mind.

"I just told you now, didn't I?"

"Chels." Molly leans her head on my shoulder. "What has gotten into you? If Ross Grunner ever texted you in the past, you always told us immediately. Why do you not even care? Don't even tell me you're over him already."

"I don't know. He doesn't seem so cute this year. I feel like his head and nose are growing faster than the rest of his body." Everyone laughs, and I take my phone out of my jacket pocket and see another text from him. I don't know why I can't just admit that I don't really like him or that I do like him as a friend, but not like that. Maybe they know what that library kid's name is, but I'd never ask them. They'd just make fun of me.

"Of course he texts *you* back and he doesn't text *me* back," Kendall says. No one responds. We're pretty much used to the fact that Kendall is in a constant competition with anyone and everyone, most of all Molly and me. So now that there's talk of Ross Grunner liking me, Kendall needs him to like her, too. She could have her own reality show: *The Kendall Competition*, but they could make the C in competition into a K to be funny.

Kendall's mom drops us off right in front of Nordstrom, and then we walk to the food court. I try as hard as I can not to be jealous of Kendall's jeans and Molly's new silver flats. I'm still wearing my old black shoes and they're a little scuffed. I wouldn't have chosen silver, I'd have chosen gold, but I'm still jealous that hers are so new and shiny and perfect.

Ross is waiting for us with the rest of the guys. They're all wearing polos and dark jeans, like a uniform.

"Hey, Chelsea," he says as soon as he sees me, and Molly pinches the top of my arm.

"Hey." I smile. Everyone's standing around us. It's the first time I've really hung out with them since I've been back at school, and it seems okay so far, but I feel like I have a running list in my brain of things I shouldn't bring up: parents, the fiftieth anniversary, Dina. If I can keep my secret throughout today, then I'll know for sure I can do it for a while.

"So, how's your new BFF?" Marcus asks me.

"Huh?" I notice Kendall pulling Ross over to the side like they're conferencing about something. I'm trying to keep an eye on them and pay attention to whatever Marcus is saying at the same time.

"Y'know, that girl you're always hanging out with." Marcus smiles. "She's been chipped, like, ten times already."

"I'm not 'always' hanging out with her," I declare, and then feel bad about saying it like she's a disease or something. "Who chipped her? You?"

"Only once by me."

I roll my eyes. "Okay, can we just stop talking about her? I'm forced to work with her and you know that."

Thankfully, Molly interrupts before I have to talk more

about Dina. "Can we please discuss who is wearing what to Cami Feldman's bat mitzvah?"

"Yes, can we please, please, please discuss?" Eric mocks her. "I have no idea what to wear. My black suit or my other black suit or my other black suit."

Molly hits him on the arm, hard. And he laughs. But you don't want to get into a fight with Molly, physical or emotional. Either way, it'll hurt.

To distract myself from the things I'm not supposed to talk about, I spend the rest of the day trying to figure out if Ross really likes me or not. Even though I don't like him that way, it's still important that he likes me. Does that make me like Kendall, always competing?

There are signs that he does: he sits next to me in the movies, he buys me a box of Sour Patch Kids (my absolute favorite candy), and he asks me how things are going at school like he really actually cares and isn't just trying to be annoying about me working with Dina, the way everyone else is.

But there are also signs that he's just being like every other boy, the way he stops a conversation midsentence to say some dumb line from *The Simpsons* to Marcus and Eric even though it has absolutely nothing to do with what we're talking about. And he spends as much time talking to me as he does whispering with Kendall off to the side.

And I could be imagining it, but it seems like when they're talking, they're always looking at me. Maybe I'm just paranoid, but I spend the whole day on pins and needles instead of having fun.

It didn't used to be like this. I used to be the one in the middle of conversations, the one people were off to the side with.

If I were on *Sasha Says So* and I could ask Sasha Preston for advice, that's what I'd ask: how to keep things the same, how to make things go back to normal, how to keep a secret without freaking out.

Maybe if Dina really does find her, I can ask her that. Maybe Sasha's just the person who can help me sort things out. Just the thought of that makes me feel better—like thinking about it will actually make it happen. Yeah, right. But I get so excited anyway. I guess being excited can't really hurt anything.

On the way home in Molly's mom's car, Molly turns around in the front seat. "Hey, Chels, you gotta see this." She hands me her phone, and it's on the video camera screen. "Just hit Play," she says.

So I do and it opens up into a video of our school cafeteria. Kendall and Molly are laughing in the background, and then it turns into a shot of Dina at her lunch table. No one's talking, and Dina's eating a bag of mini-carrots, crunching and crunching, staring into space. Then the video ends, and I hand Molly back her phone.

"What do you think?" Molly asks.

I say, "Um . . . it's a video of Dina eating carrots?"

Molly's mom stays silent during this whole thing, clicking her nails on her fancy wooden steering wheel.

"Isn't it funny?" Kendall screeches. "See, we can take videos, too!"

Molly and Kendall crack up, and I guess it is kind of funny, actually, and it's not really mean or anything—it's just a video of her eating carrots. Everyone eats carrots.

"We're so putting it on Facebook," Molly says. "It'll be really funny."

"No, come on," I say. "Really?"

"Don't be lame, Chelsea," Molly says. "Or I'm telling Ross."

I don't know what to say, so I just say nothing and hope that they forget about this.

DINA

Video tip: Avoid talking heads. Shoot a lot of
B-roll so you don't bore your audience.

Nathan is so lucky to be in fourth grade. It's not even
a big deal for fourth graders to start a new school, and they
obviously don't have to worry about chipping.

Also, all the third and fourth graders in Rockwood Hills
are on soccer teams. It's a coed league, and it's a huge deal. So
of course my parents had to sign him up for one. They made
sure to do that before we even moved here.

My mom is always on top of this stuff.

So Nathan has built-in plans on Saturdays. He's getting
ready to leave for his soccer game, all geared up in his cleats
and his shin guards. All I want at this minute is to be a
fourth-grade boy. Seriously.

Because right now my mom is doing that thing that she

does. She asks me what my plans are for the day when she knows I don't have any. It didn't used to be like this. She didn't used to have to ask because I always had plans.

"You could call someone," she says, all casual.

"Who should I call, Mom?" I don't look up from my laptop when I talk to her. Making eye contact would only make things worse.

"What about that girl that you're working with on that project? You said she was very nice, and popular, too. And didn't you say she lives in the Pine section of the neighborhood?"

Our neighborhood is divided into four sections. Each of them has a tree name. So Chelsea lives in the Pine section and we live in the Elm section. Everyone knows the Pine section is the fanciest and the Spruce section is the least fancy, mostly because it backs the expressway. The Elm section is one step above Spruce because it doesn't back the expressway and the houses are bigger, plus that's where the neighborhood pool is. People in the Pine section have their own pools. Some of them, anyway. The Maple section is right below the Pine section, and some of the houses are actually bigger, just not as new or fancy.

"Yeah, she does. I'm not calling her, though, Mom. So please don't even think about it."

"Dina," she says in that tone that leads me to believe that whatever comes next is going to be impossible to say no to.

"You have to make an effort. You're the new one. Please just call her."

"She has a million friends, Mom," I say, ending the round of the computer version of Connect Four. "She doesn't need me. We're just working on the project together, and she doesn't even want to be working on it, really. We're not BFFs." I pause and wait for her to say something, but she doesn't. "It's different here," I say under my breath.

My mom sits next to me on the couch and closes the laptop. "First of all, it's very rude to be on the computer when someone is trying to talk to you. Second of all, how do you know she doesn't need another friend? You can never have too many friends. And besides, what's the worst that can happen?"

"The worst that can happen is that she tells all her friends how I called for plans and everyone knows how pathetic I really am." I get up from the couch and walk into the kitchen for a snack. "Just forget about it. Go with Nathan to his soccer game. I'll be fine here."

"You can at least come with us to his soccer game." My mom follows me into the kitchen. She doesn't understand the term *personal space*.

I grab a handful of almonds. "No way. Then if by chance anyone from school is there, they'll know how pathetic I am that I didn't even have plans so I had to tag along with my parents to my younger brother's soccer game."

"Well, if they're at the game, they must be pathetic, too, right?" My mom leans onto the island in the kitchen. She has a look on her face like she's just so smart.

"No, because I bet they'll be there with someone else." I clench my teeth. My mother has to be the most infuriating person in the world. I'm sorry it pains her so much that I don't have any friends, but it was her idea to move us here. If we were back home, I'd be with Ali right now. We'd be planning our outfits for the next two weeks and drinking iced tea on her back patio.

"Either call the girl or come with us to the game," my mom insists. "One or the other. But I'm not leaving you here alone."

"I'm thirteen years old, Mom. I can handle staying home alone."

"Stop talking back to me, Dina."

"Fine, I'll call Chelsea, but leave the room, please." I don't know why I think this is a good plan. Clearly, she's not going to leave the room. And I could have made it much simpler by leaving the room myself and pretending to call upstairs. Sometimes I just don't think things through.

"I won't listen. Just call her."

"I'll go upstairs."

"Dina. Call her now."

My mom is a half a minute away from screaming. I do not want her to scream. Because then my dad will get involved, and he'll be mad at me. Nathan will be late to his game, and it will all be my fault.

I take my cell phone out of my jeans pocket and dial Chelsea's number. The only reason I have it is because Mr. Valakis made us exchange numbers so we'd be prepared to work on the project together. Rockwood Hills Middle School isn't the kind of school to have a phone directory, and I wouldn't have one anyway since I came a month late.

Please don't be home. Please don't be home. Please don't be home, I pray. And then I realize how dumb I am because even if she isn't home this is her cell phone number. *Please don't answer. Please don't answer. Please don't answer.*

"Hello?" a male voice answers on the fourth ring.

A male voice? On her cell phone? Does she have a boyfriend? Or is this her dad answering her phone? I absolutely forbid my parents from answering my phone, and they obey my request. Usually.

"Um, hi, is Chelsea there?"

"No, she's at the movies with her friends." A pause. "Who's this?"

Oh, God, clearly this person knows I'm not her friend, because if I was her friend, I'd be at the movies with her. And everyone else. So who am I talking to? And why doesn't Chelsea have her cell phone with her? Why did my mom make me do this? And why is my life so unbelievably embarrassing?

"Oh, um, I'm Dina." I swallow hard and debate just hanging up.

"Did you try her cell?"

"I thought this was her cell?" I say and feel even worse than before. What is worse than an utter living hell? Whatever it is, I'm experiencing it.

"No, this is the home line." Pause again. "I'll tell her Dina called, though. She should be—"

"No, that's okay," I interrupt. "Um, thanks. Bye."

I hang up while he's still sort of half-talking, something like *Are you sure?*

"So?" my mom asks. I was so focused on how absolutely awful the call was that I forgot my mom was still in the kitchen.

"Don't ask." I squint even though it's not even sunny in here and try as hard as I can to keep from crying. "I'll go get my sweatshirt and meet you guys in the car."

"Dina. You're my daughter. I know when you're about to cry," she says as I'm already out of the kitchen and in the hallway.

She's right. She does know. And I do cry. Up in my room,

into my pillow, like some pathetic girl who doesn't get what she wants. But I'm not pathetic. I just don't have any friends here, and now even Chelsea's dad knows that.

And Chelsea's at the movies with all those girls who did the "Sea-Sea Stern" cheer during badminton, and I bet Ross and all the boys that sit at the table next to them during lunch are there, too. And I bet they're all slurping Cherry Cokes and eating mega bags of popcorn with greasy liquid butter. And they're all laughing and wearing their cropped leggings and their long cardigans. All of the girls' hair is straight and perfect and they look like models from the Delia's catalog.

And I'm at home wearing last season's Gap jeans with a zip-up sweater I got for Hanukkah two years ago. And I won't be going to the movies. I'll be going to my brother's stupid Rockwood Hills Soccer League game, where I'll probably see other kids from school.

Not the Chelsea Sterns but the Katherine Fellsons and the Maura Eastlys, the girls who aren't popular, who live in the Spruce section. The girls who are just normal, who don't worry about being seen at their brothers' soccer games because they have friends.

I suppose I could try to be friends with them. They let me sit with them at lunch. They're acceptable. They'd probably welcome me more than Chelsea would. But I don't want to. I don't want to be someone who just fades into the background, someone who's friends with people by default.

"Dina," my mom yells to me from downstairs. "Come on. Now. We're going. Nathan's going to be late."

"Coming," I yell back. I can't believe this is how today's turning out.

Forget this. Forget trying so hard to be friends with someone who doesn't want me. I never thought I'd be someone like that. I don't want to be that person. I don't want to be so desperate. I'm changing my mind. I'm going to become friends with Katherine and Maura. It will be fine. Katherine and Maura are fine. They're more than fine; they're good enough at least. There are extra seats at their lunch table. And they let me sit there.

They accept me. I accept them. They're the Acceptables.

And that's all I really need right now.

CHELSEA

Sasha Preston piece of advice: If you're
tired, wear something red.

My parents always used to be the type to go out
on Saturday nights. Fancy places, too. My mom would wear
nice pants or a dress, and my dad would wear a shirt and
jacket and sometimes a tie.

Lately, not so much.

And I can tell my mom wants to go out because she'll
drop not-so-subtle hints like, "The Cohens are going to
Riverbay on Saturday. They said we're welcome to join
them." Or "The Steinfelds have a subscription to this off-
Broadway show series. We can get discount tickets."

In the beginning, my dad would go along with it. Up
until about a month ago, he'd even still go out to the fanciest

restaurants and order bottles of wine, and it seemed like nothing had really changed at all.

Until mid-September. It was like he flicked a switch, or someone flicked a switch for him. That's when he started working out for hours and staying in his workout clothes all day and making every day feel like every other day.

These are the cues I hate, the cues that tell me things are bad and getting worse, and they make me wonder how bad things will end up getting. I wonder what rock bottom is and when we'll hit it. And I'm scared of what will happen when we do.

I was happy to be sleeping at Kendall's on Saturday night just so I could get away from it, but even though I wasn't home, all the feelings were still there. They were stuck at the back of my brain, and as hard as I tried to get rid of them, they stayed stuck.

Even all the talk about Ross Grunner wasn't getting my mind off of things at home. And it was good talk, too. Molly and Kendall convinced me that Ross really does like me, and they tried to convince me that I really like him, too.

So I called him and we talked for forty-one minutes, and it was a good conversation that flowed normally. We decided we'd hang out one day after school, and he even offered to help with the video. He's good with that kind of stuff. And truthfully, it would be good to have some help and to have another person to work with us. Being one-on-one with Dina for that long can make you crazy after a while.

There were even parts of the night when I felt like I could maybe open up to them about stuff, and maybe it wouldn't be so weird. They were my friends, after all, and they liked me, so they'd understand.

But then they'd say something like how sad it was that AJ Marcuzzi had to move away because his house was going into foreclosure. But they didn't say it like they were sad and they felt bad for them—they talked about it more in a gossipy way. I know for sure they heard their parents gossiping about it just the same way.

And I joined in on the conversation saying, yeah, it was sad and all of that. Because as long as they didn't know the truth about me, then I was just like them, the way I always was.

And at least they didn't bring up the carrot video again.

So now it's Monday morning and I'm sitting in homeroom, feeling tired and thinking too hard. All my friends and I are in the same homeroom this year. At first, I thought this was a good thing, but now I'm beginning to think it's not. They surround me.

"Chels, you seemed so quiet on Saturday," Molly says. "We all want to talk to you about it."

And Kendall says, "We're very worried about you. You have to talk to us."

"Guys, I'm fine." I laugh a little to prove my point.

"Yeah, right," Kendall says. "You didn't even freak out about Ross Grunner."

"Guys," I say again, looking around to make sure he's not listening to us. "I mean, what's there to say? We'll see what happens."

He's sitting in the back of the room, wearing a gray button-down and dark jeans. His hair's always a little messed up on top, but I know he tries to get it to look that way. Some girls think that's cute. I'm not sure.

"Okay, quiet, quiet, quiet," Mrs. Feder says, already sounding annoyed as she walks into the classroom. "Attendance, and then silent homeroom. It's way too early for all this noise."

She says this every morning. Homeroom is always the same time, so it's obviously *always* too early for all that noise. But today I'm actually thankful for Mrs. Feder because it means I don't have to talk to my friends.

Which is kind of sad, actually.

After homeroom I'm walking to math when I spot Dina. I

don't know what to do. Should I say anything about how she called my house? My dad told me about it when I got home on Sunday. He's really good at giving messages, especially now that he never really leaves the house.

Dina's looking down as she walks past. I can't tell if she's trying to avoid me or not. I didn't call her back, mostly because I didn't really have much to say. The weekend had been so tough, even the excitement about Sasha Preston had worn off.

She looks up for half a second and our eyes meet, and I casually wave, but no words come out of my mouth.

She probably thinks I hate her. I may not like her, but I don't think I hate her. At least, I don't want her to think I hate her.

I'll talk to her at lunch. That's what I'll do. I'll just casually tap her on the shoulder on the lunch line and say that my dad didn't give me the message until really late last night and I wasn't sure how late I could call her house. Yeah, that works. I'll say that my dad is really bad with messages. She doesn't need to know the truth. It's not like she's ever going to come over to my house. At least, I hope not.

But when lunch rolls around, I see her walking around the cafeteria with the video camera again, and I'm too nervous about what my friends are going to say if go up and talk to her. So I don't do anything.

Maybe she forgot that I didn't call her back—maybe it just slipped her mind. That could happen.

But to make up for it, I get to the library a little early and get out all the yearbooks, even the ones behind Mr. Singer's desk. And I get her a bag of Peanut M&M's from the vending machine.

The library helper hasn't been here since last week. He must help out other places or something. Or maybe he's finished with his community service requirement for the semester. I get all my community service hours picking up trash in the park around the corner from my house. You'd be surprised at how many people litter. It's pretty shocking how much trash there is even after I've cleaned it all up just the day before.

I don't know why I'm going so out of my way to be nice to Dina. I guess it's because I feel bad, or maybe I just feel like it's one thing I can kind of control in my life. And I feel like it's one good, positive thing that I can do. I don't feel so bad lying to my friends if I'm nice to Dina. It's a ridiculous theory, but it makes sense in my head. And the thing is, I don't have to worry about Dina liking me—I know she does, so it's one less thing to worry about.

Wow. Since when did I become a psychoanalyst? That came out of nowhere.

"Hey," I say to Dina as she's walking in. I'm a little loud

for the library, but I want to get her attention. Luckily, Mr. Singer doesn't say anything.

"Oh, hi. You're early," she says.

"And I brought you Peanut M&M's." I hand her the bag and pat the chair next to me, motioning for her to sit down.

"Thanks so much," she says.

"Did you have a good weekend?" I ask her, and then regret it because now she's going to bring up the fact that I didn't call her back.

She shrugs. "It was kind of boring. I had to go to my brother's soccer game. You have a sister, right? Does she play in the league?"

"Yeah, she's in fourth grade. I think she's on the Super Stoppers this year."

"My brother, too. I mean, about the fourth-grade thing. I have no idea what team he's on. They all sound the same to me."

I roll my eyes. "Yeah, that soccer league stuff is nutso. The parents think they're, like, training Olympians or something. My dad used to coach." I pause. Why, why, why did I just bring up my dad? She's going to ask me why he doesn't coach anymore.

Dina nods. "Did he get too fed up with the politics to continue? I feel like that happened all the time where I used to live."

"Um, yeah." I swallow hard. "So, anyway, I was looking at the yearbooks over the weekend. And I think I uncovered something!" My voice comes out more excited-sounding than I actually feel at this moment.

"Really? What?" Dina pops an M&M in her mouth and moves her chair closer to mine. Her hair smells like papaya or some other fruit, and it reminds me of the shampoo my counselors used at camp. I get a sudden sad feeling, wishing so much that it was still July.

"Something happened to Sasha when she was at this school. She went from having friends to not having friends." I open the yearbook. "Here, look at this. In her seventh-grade yearbook, Sasha Preston had lots of friends. Like, a *lot* of them. They wrote messages to each other and everything. And in the sixth grade, too. But then in eighth grade, nothing. It was like she was a total loner—no friends, no messages. How did everything just change like that?"

We sit and look through the yearbooks as closely as we can, especially the ones from when Sasha was in sixth and seventh grades. We look up all the friends she was in pictures with and then look them up in the eighth-grade one to find them.

"So they all still lived here and went to this school," Dina says. "She wasn't a loner because all her friends moved away."

"Yeah, they were all still here."

"So what could have happened? Look, no secret messages to each other in this one. She doesn't even have an eighth-grade testimonial section. It's just totally blank under her name." Dina mushes up her face like she feels really bad for Sasha. I don't know why—her life certainly turned out okay.

"Here's my theory. What if she was a really bad friend? Like, she stole the boy her best friend was in love with for years?" I ask. I don't want to talk to Dina about the whole Ross Grunner thing and Kendall. I can't let her in on all the drama with them.

"You think she'd do that?"

"No idea," I say. "I mean, it probably happens a lot. More than we realize." *Stop, Chelsea, stop!* I don't know why I can't keep my mouth shut.

"It's never happened to me," Dina admits. "My best friend, Ali, and I had fake crushes. We picked guys we didn't really know at all. We never, like, planned to do anything about our crushes. But my old school was kind of innocent like that."

"What do you mean 'innocent'?" I ask. The way she's describing it, it sounds like she grew up Amish or something. But I know she didn't, because I saw her at Hebrew School registration at the end of the summer, even though I had no idea who she was at the time.

"Boys and girls didn't hang out. Or go out." She looks down at the yearbook. "Clearly, I don't know what I'm talking about."

Suddenly, Dina's all nervous, and I have no idea why.

"Wait, so you've never really liked a guy?"

She starts chewing on the inside of her cheek. "I have. I just never expected anything to happen. And now it definitely won't since I moved away." She sighs. "So, you mean to say that people steal their friends' crushes all the time here?"

"No. I guess sometimes. But not all the time." I clench my teeth. I don't want to say anything else.

Dina's about to say something else when I see Mr. Valakis out of the corner of my eye. "We need to look busy," I tell her under my breath. "Mr. Valakis."

"So, we have about twenty minutes of strong footage," Dina starts. "We need to get more, and focus on the direction we want to go, and then streamline the whole thing."

Wow, she's good. She should be an actress or a spy. I don't know where she got that from, but it sounded so believable and I really wish it were true.

"Hi, girls," Mr. Valakis says. "I was looking for you. I just want to get a sense of your progress—so we can help you if we need to. You still have some more class time to work on this, but, as you know, it's hard to get good material when classes are in session."

"Uh-huh." Dina smiles.

"So?"

"We're working on it, Mr. Valakis," I say.

"I'm just looking for some kind of progress report here," he says, sounding a bit confused.

"Oh, we're doing fine," Dina says. "But you know how it is when you're in the thick of a project. It's hard to discuss it with people."

I cover my mouth and try as hard as I can not to crack up. *The thick of a project?* Where does she get this stuff?

"Well, I'll need to see something soon. Next week or the week after, at the latest. Good luck, girls."

He walks away.

"Next week?" I say.

"Whoa."

"We've got serious work to do."

"I know." She looks at me like she's debating about saying something, not sure if she should or not. "But I have to ask you something."

Oh, no. She's heard a rumor. That's what someone says when they've heard a rumor and they want to know if it's true or not. It's all happening, everything's falling apart, and it feels like it just snuck up on me. "What?" I ask tentatively.

"Why didn't you call me back?" She crumples up the

M&M's wrapper in her hand. "Because in my old school people called me back. In my old school, I was actually someone that people liked." She stops talking, probably because she realizes how pathetic she sounds.

"I just forgot." I can't look at her right now. She's this really weird combination of bold and insecure, and I don't get it. She'll just call me out on things that I do, but at the same time it's so obvious that she's desperate to be my friend. "Okay? Can we just move on and focus on the video?"

"I have it under control." She packs up her notebook and her cool pens and ties her hair back into a low ponytail. "Okay?" She mocks me but not in a cruel way.

As we walk out of the library, I realize that I hate her a little bit less than I used to, and I think it's because she just said that she has it under control. That's all I really want, to have things under control.

The project keeps my mind off of everything else, and I like that.

And when I'm nice to her, I just feel the tiniest bit better about things.

DINA

Video tip: Cut shorter as opposed to longer.
People get bored by long interviews.

"Stop staring at him, Maura," Katherine says, flicking a piece of macaroni off the table. "He's such a jerk."

"I know he's a jerk, but a jerk can still be cute."

We're at lunch, and the Acceptables are talking about what they always talk about: Chelsea and her friends and Ross. It's either that or what test they have to study for. But I try not to complain about it or think about how boring they are, because they're all I've got. And they're actually not that bad. We've been sitting together for a couple of weeks already. I'm used to it.

"Chelsea Stern has the perfect life," Maura says. "It's like she doesn't even try at all to get Ross Grunner to talk to her."

"I know. And she doesn't even look excited when he does

talk to her. And he talks to her, like, all the time," Katherine says. "It's not even a big deal to her."

I just sit there quietly eating my lunch and observing this conversation. I should probably say something, but I have no idea what to add.

"You're working on that video project with her, right?" Trisha asks.

I nod.

"The thing about Chelsea Stern," she goes on, "is that you really want to hate her, but you just can't. She's not mean like that Molly creature. Molly isn't even human."

"I really don't know her well at all," I admit. "You may be right, though. We didn't have that kind of creature back in Massachusetts."

The whole table laughs, and for the first time since I've been sitting with them, I feel happy with where I am.

Soon they're asking me all these questions about life in the Berkshires, and I tell them about going to concerts at Tanglewood and sitting on the grass and getting to meet all these famous musicians since my dad was the head of finance there. I tell them about being able to ski all winter long. And as I'm talking, I realize how much I miss it.

But even as I say all of this, and feel okay about being friends with these girls, I realize they're all totally fake, saying this stuff about how awful Molly is. Because the truth is they all want to be friends with her and Chelsea and Kendall as much as I do.

Lunch is almost over, and I can't waste an opportunity to get some footage for the video. Mr. Valakis is serious about wanting to see progress. And we haven't made much.

"I'm gonna get some footage," I tell the table. They look at me confused and kind of scared.

"Here?" Trisha asks. "In the cafeteria?"

I shrug. "Sure."

They nod, like kids who are waiting in line to go on a roller coaster after their parents ask them if they really want to go.

I try to ignore their fear and just get up. There's so much hubbub, what with people walking around, throwing out their food, scrounging up extra change for an ice cream, that I doubt anyone will notice me.

I just walk around, getting shots of people at the garbage cans, at their tables, finishing last bites of their lunches.

"Hey, video fanatic!" I hear Kendall yell, and I take that as a positive sign. I walk over to their table.

"Hey," I say to them, still filming.

"Why are you doing this?" Molly says, shouting so loud that the tables around us turn to look at me.

"For the thingie—you know, the fiftieth-anniversary event." I smile with the camera still on. I'm not going to let her get to me. If I act cool and calm and relaxed, then she won't bother me. "Just trying to get some casual cafeteria shots."

The whole table cracks up, definitely in a laughing-*at*-me kind of way. I smile again and keep shooting. I like being behind the camera; it feels natural. In a way, I feel protected by it, like no one can really bother me while I'm filming, because whatever they do will be captured forever on video.

It's odd but comforting.

Ross Grunner comes over from the boys' table and stands behind me looking at the display screen of the camera. "Good work," Ross says and pats me on the shoulder. "I can't wait to watch it."

I smile. Does he really mean that? I can't tell what type of shots I'm getting. I'm just proud of myself for having the confidence to walk around the cafeteria.

But then, just as I'm leaving the cafeteria, Molly trips me. It's so obvious that she's going to do it, too, so I don't even really fall, I just stumble and drop the camera. Luckily, it bounces a little on the rubbery linoleum floor and doesn't break.

"You probably have enough *casual cafeteria shots*," she says, totally mocking me.

I pick up the camera, and say, "Thanks, Molly. I'm grateful for your editorial input."

Chelsea calls me later that night. Apparently, miracles do happen. At first, I assume she's going to say something about the tripping incident, but she doesn't.

"How's the Sasha search going? Are you going to sign up for one of those services that tell you who her agent is?" she asks me.

"No, those sites are total scams," I tell her, wondering why she's suddenly so intrigued with the project. "I told you—I can find her myself. Celebrities are on Twitter all the time saying where they are. It's not that hard. I'm looking right now, actually."

"Okay, if you say so . . . Actually, hold on a sec," Chelsea tells me.

While she's gone, I click all around the Internet searching for Sasha Preston stuff. A lot of it is fan pages and random sites about people obsessing over her. So weird. Imagine if I had people obsessing over me. I bet it would be kind of awesome in the beginning but would start to get kind of awkward after a while.

In the background at Chelsea's house, I hear yelling. At first, I think it's a joke or maybe people yelling at a TV during some kind of sporting event. But then I realize it's actual, serious yelling.

I can't totally make out what the people are saying, but suddenly I can. A woman's voice says, "You need to fix this! I can't live like this anymore!"

And then the male voice says, "I don't see you making any changes!"

Too bad Chelsea didn't put me on hold. This is awkward. I wonder if I should pretend that I didn't hear anything. Or ask Chelsea if she's okay. That is, if she ever comes back to the phone. What if she just leaves me waiting forever? When should I hang up?

I take a break from my Sasha Preston searching and try to do a little searching on Chelsea's parents. Maybe if I knew a little more about the situation, I'd know why they're fighting and I could help more.

Do most people Google their friends on a regular basis? Probably not.

Do I care? Not at all. If I don't become a movie director, I'll probably become a detective or an investigative journalist. I just like finding out stuff about people. And it's always more exciting if it's stuff I really shouldn't know.

I don't know what Chelsea's parents' names are, so I go to the Rockwood Hills Middle School website and search for last year's PTA Ball. One of the Acceptables mentioned that her mom was in charge of it.

I pull up a link to photos from the event, and at the very top are Chelsea's parents.

They're beautiful people. They're old and stuff, but they still look good. I hope I'm like that when I'm old and a parent.

Bruce and Dayna Stern.

I copy/paste that into Google.

Nothing comes up except for pages having to do with Rockwood Hills Middle School.

I can't believe Chelsea hasn't come back to the phone yet. I feel like I should hang up, but I'm not sure. I put my phone on speaker and lay it on my desk. It's hard to type and hold a phone at the same time.

I type "Bruce Stern" into Google and get a million hits.

I type "Bruce Stern Long Island" into Google and get a lot fewer.

This stuff pops up about one of the most successful investment bankers in the New York area. "Worked for the same bank for over twenty years." "Bruce Stern, one of the brightest minds in the banking industry."

"Hi, Dina, sorry." Chelsea's back on the phone just as I find the missing clue: "Bruce Stern let go—A shock to the industry."

"Hi." My voice is crackly.

I hear the voices of Trisha, Maura, and Katherine in my head. *Chelsea Stern has the perfect life.* Obviously, she doesn't. Obviously, things aren't always what they seem.

I have no idea what to do now.

"So did you find her yet?" Chelsea asks.

"Um—I'm getting closer, I think." I feel like I can't speak. I don't know what to say. I wish I hadn't been so nosy and searched for her parents. Why did I think Googling her dad would be a good idea? "I gotta go, Chelsea. Sorry! My mom is mad at me for being on the phone so much."

"You're on the phone so much?" Chelsea asks like that's really hard to believe. I try not to get too offended. After all, she's going through a lot. "With who?"

"Well, yeah, with my old friends and stuff. See you tomorrow. Meet in the library after school?"

"Yeah," she says. "Well, I'll see you in social studies anyway."

"Right."

"G'night."

"Night."

I'm still holding the phone after we hang up because I'm so shocked about this thing with her parents. Does anyone else know about this? People lose their jobs all the time, but it seems like it would be a big deal for Chelsea Stern.

I sign into Gmail so I can quickly video-chat with Ali before bed. She said she has a lot to tell me about the benefit at Tanglewood this past weekend. She said all sorts of people were there—Susan Sarandon and Bruce Willis and Oprah.

Ali's dad worked with my dad there, and we would go to all the benefits together. We'd get dressed up and schmooze with classical musicians like Yo-Yo Ma.

See, I should play that up more when I talk to Rockwood Hills people. I should have been doing that from the beginning. But I didn't want to appear arrogant and artsy in a snobby way.

As soon as I click into Gmail, I see that I have Facebook friend requests. It's too bad real life can't be more like Facebook. You can't just request for someone to be your friend and then they will be. Life would be much easier if it was like that.

But these aren't any old friend requests—they're from Kendall Rogers and Molly Settlen! Maybe they felt bad about the cafeteria incident earlier today. Maybe they're realizing I really am cool. I didn't get frazzled, and I didn't let them see me upset. Maybe they know that Chelsea's calling me now, and that's making them like me, too.

I quickly accept their friend requests and then click open the video-chat from Ali.

She tells me all about the Tanglewood event, the turquoise dress she wore, how Isaac Mizrahi complimented her on it, and how she thinks she can get accepted into the Boston junior symphony orchestra.

But it's too hard to focus on all of that after I've just uncovered something big, something about Chelsea, something I'm not sure I should tell anyone.

And everything that Ali is saying sounds great, but for the first time I'm not sitting here wishing I was there. I'm too happy about the call from Chelsea and the friend requests from Kendall and Molly to be doing that.

For the first time I'm actually kind of excited about going to school tomorrow.

12

CHELSEA

Sasha Preston piece of advice: Have
an open mind. It's easier than it seems.

I think I finally figured out why I'm kind of enjoying
working on this project. The reason is pretty simple: it takes
my mind off things.

When I'm home, I'm obviously thinking about how
horrible things are there, how bad I feel for both my parents,
and how I wish things could just go back to the way they used
to be. And I'm constantly imagining how bad things could
end up getting: selling the house, having to move into a tiny
apartment somewhere, and having to change schools since
there are no apartment buildings in Rockwood Hills.

And when I'm with my friends, all they can talk about is
the stuff they're buying and getting and all I can think about
is how upset I am that I can't have that stuff.

Or they're talking about Ross Grunner. Every night Kendall calls me to talk about him. And I don't know what to say! He hasn't asked me out yet, so it's not like there's news. And I know all she wants me to say is that I don't really like him that much and that she can go after him, but why should I do that? Kendall has everything else. She was always the one who wanted what everyone else had, and now she has it. Even though I don't really even like him, she doesn't need to have him.

So I look forward to working after school with Dina because all I have to think about is the project and finding Sasha Preston, and Dina's the one with the game plan. And when I see Dina, I kind of feel better about myself. That's probably the rudest thing ever. But it's true, and I bet a lot of people feel it, even if they don't admit it.

I mean, Dina's fine, but she's just average. Average looks, average clothes, average everything. And no one knows her, except to know that's she's new and she's been chipped more times than you can count.

So when I compare myself to her, I've still got it pretty good. I used to have the best clothes. And they're still good, just not brand-new. Boys notice me. My hair never frizzes.

It may be conceited to think all of these things, but you have to be happy with what you have.

Plus the thing about Dina and me working together is that

she's so excited. At first, I thought it was kind of annoying. But now I like it. Ever since I made up for not calling her back with the Peanut M&M's, it's been smooth sailing.

She really wants to be my friend. And that feels good.

It would make anyone feel good, I think.

Mr. Valakis finds us during social studies. He looks concerned; he always looks concerned. "Girls, you still haven't shown me any progress on your video," he says.

"You just asked us," I say. "With all due respect, true art takes time to mold." I don't know how those words just came out of my mouth. It must be Dina's influence, but I actually kind of like it.

He pinches his lips together. "I see."

"We're really working hard," Dina adds. "It's just there's a lot in the works and we can't reveal it yet."

I kick her under the table. She shouldn't have said that. It sounds like we're up to no good.

"Well, I really need to be kept in the loop," he says. "This is a huge event, and everyone there will be seeing your work. I can't have you turning out something like you'd see on MTV." He laughs nervously.

"That would actually be kind of cool," Dina says. "A music video—like a theme song for the school. All good slide shows and montages are put to music. And with all due respect, Mr.

Valakis, many of the music videos you see are highly cinematic and well thought out."

Is she serious right now?

"At least you're putting some thought into it. That's a start." He gives us a thumbs-up and walks away.

Dina takes her glasses off and cleans them with the sleeve of her long-sleeve Ben & Jerry's tie-dyed T-shirt. Tie-dyed? Seriously? "Well, I'm gonna run to the bathroom," she says. "Why don't you start taping? Maybe some footage of kids in this class, just working on their projects?"

Dina gets up, asks Mr. Valakis if she can go, and leaves the room.

"Is she kidding with that shirt?" Kendall asks as she moves her chair closer to mine. As soon as Dina's gone, they completely drop their own project and come bug me. "I mean, really, is she kidding?"

I shake my head. "I don't think so."

Molly picks the camera up off Dina's desk and starts fiddling with it, pushing the red Record button and taping herself and then panning around the room to tape everyone else.

"It's kind of weird to see life through a video camera," she says. "Doesn't that sound so, like, deep?"

Kendall bulges her eyes out at Molly. "Real deep, Molls. We'll just call you Aristotle."

I'm a little impressed Kendall knows who Aristotle is, so I smile along with her.

Molly's still holding the camera when Dina comes back into the room. She saunters back in, all dramatic. But what she doesn't realize is that she has a train of toilet paper stuck to her shoe. She must've dragged it all the way down the hallway from the bathroom.

She's oblivious, like she always is, and then things go from bad to worse.

She trips. It's not like anyone spilled anything or there are wires or things on the floor. She just trips for no reason. She uses her hands to break her fall, and the toilet paper gets tangled around her ankle, which totally grosses everyone out.

And then the class starts chanting, "Gross Gross, gross Gross!"

It is kind of unfortunate that her last name is Gross. No one in the world would want that as a last name. If she becomes a famous movie director, like she plans to, she'll have to change it.

"Stop!" Mr. Valakis yells. He's not really a yeller, so this sounds really abnormal coming from him. The class totally quiets down immediately. "Dina, are you okay?"

"Oh, I'm fine." She laughs, and gets up and then curtsies, like she finds the whole thing funny and isn't embarrassed at all. I think Dina's pretty much impossible to embarrass.

Mr. Valakis delivers a lecture on a time he dropped a

tray of food in his high school's cafeteria and how laughing at someone is very detrimental and blah blah blah. I'm not listening because I'm reading a note from Ross.

hey chelsers. when are we hanging out?

It's not a long note, but I read it over and over again trying to decipher what it means. Maybe he really wants to know when we're hanging out? But if he really wants to hang out so much, why doesn't he suggest a day?

Why can't boys just reveal what's on their mind, and then girls would never have to wonder and stress? Or maybe boys' brains could have some kind of ticker, like on the bottom of the TV screen when you're watching CNN—that would be great, too.

After Mr. Valakis's lecture on human kindness or whatever, Dina asks, "So, get any cool footage while I was gone?"

I shake my head. Dina's camera's back on her desk, but when I lean over and look at Molly's MacBook, I see a video of Dina falling on the screen.

Molly must've transferred the whole thing while Mr. Valakis was lecturing us.

How does Molly know so much about using a video camera all of a sudden?

"Let's get more B-roll after school—but random people

shots," Dina says. "We'll meet in the library and walk around and we'll see who we find." She waits for me to speak, but I'm still trying to not focus on what's happening on Molly's computer screen.

Ross hands me another note, and I get excited, but when I look at the front of the folded piece of paper, it says *for dina*.

First, he just goes up and talks to her in the cafeteria, and now he's writing her notes.

I hand it to Dina, and she squeals, "A note? For me?" like some kind of damsel in an old-fashioned movie.

She doesn't read it aloud, and she doesn't show it to me, but a few seconds later she turns back to Ross and says, "Sure!"

I can't imagine what Ross would write on a note to Dina, especially after she just totally humiliated herself in front of the class. Maybe it's some witty tip on how to walk without tripping. That'd be a very Ross thing to do.

The bell rings, and I leave social studies with this anxious, nervous feeling, like there's a handful of half-chewed red hots sitting in my stomach. I don't like that there's a video of Dina falling on Molly's computer, and I don't like that Ross passed her a note. And I especially don't like that I don't know what that note said.

13

DINA

Video tip: Comedy comes in threes.

Now that I know about Chelsea's dad, I want her to tell me. I feel guilty knowing it, because she didn't tell me herself. I wonder who else knows. Definitely not the Acceptables, because if they knew, they'd stop saying that she has the perfect life.

Today at lunch they were going on and on about where she gets her hair cut and how you have to make an appointment at least three months in advance.

"My mom went there once," Trisha said. "It was for my cousin's communion. It's not like she goes there every single month, like Chelsea's mom."

I didn't know what to say.

I'm going to put the whole thing about Chelsea's dad out of my head until she tells me. And I'm going to try to focus on the positive: Chelsea actually seems to care about this project now, or at least she did on the phone the other day.

After school I'm sitting at the back table, our usual meeting spot in the library, when someone taps me on the shoulder. "Hey, hey," I say, and then look up. It's not Chelsea. It's Ross. I immediately feel really dumb for saying "Hey, hey." I should've known it would be him because he asked if he could come by and help. I can't believe I forgot.

He mimics me and says it right back.

"So video me!" He sits down in the sturdy wooden library chair and rocks back, so it's only resting on two of the legs. "Shoot."

I laugh. "How do you even know about this?"

"Chelsea was talking about it the other day," he says. "And you think I don't notice you walking around school with that camera? Come on."

I laugh again. It's interesting to know that Chelsea was talking about it. That means things are going even better than I thought. I take out the camera and zoom in on Ross's face. He has a tiny group of freckles on the bridge of his nose but nowhere else. It seems like he has a permanent tan.

He's cute. No wonder the Acceptables talk about him all the time.

"Ready?" he asks.

"I really wanted to just get candid shots," I tell him. "Like people doing their thing."

"Oh, I know," he says. "So tape me doing my thing—studying. Ha!"

So I hit Record, and he's just sitting here looking at a book with this stupid grin on his face. It makes me crack up. And then after a little while he just starts talking. "I'm proud to say I've only been chipped once, and that was when I was in sixth grade and my brother Jake was in eighth. He chipped me. Being chipped by a sibling doesn't count." He stops talking. I wait for him to start again but he doesn't.

"What was that all about?" I ask.

"I wanted to state my case on being chipped. I am not a victim!" He laughs.

"True. You've been chipped much less than I have, and I've only been here a month."

He pats my shoulder. I squirm away a little bit without meaning to.

After Ross leaves, I'm alone in the library, and I start to think about this whole chipping concept. Who was the first person to decide it was cool to mush potato chips into someone's bag? I wonder how long it's been going on. Maybe if we ever find Sasha Preston, we can ask her about that.

I push the Play button and watch Ross's video. He has

extremely straight teeth and this funny, crooked smile with one side of his mouth much higher than the other. He kind of looks like a miniature George Clooney. Well, not miniature. A younger, shorter George Clooney. A very cute miniature George Clooney.

After the video ends, I'm about to shut the camera off when I see that there's another video I haven't seen. And it's of me! When I open it, I see myself tripping in the doorway to social studies.

I guess Chelsea left the camera on by mistake. I quickly hit Delete to get rid of it. Good thing I saw it.

"We got our first actual good clip!" I tell Chelsea as soon as she arrives, ten minutes late.

"Who? What? Where?" She drops her bag and sits down and looks around like she's expecting someone else to be here. The faux fur on her coat is rubbing against her cheeks. They're all red, like she's been outside in the cold for hours.

"Ross." I lift my hand for a high five, but she denies me. But I go on anyway. "He wanted me to tape him studying, and then he just went on this rant about chipping."

She laughs. "You mean, being chipped? No one says *chipping*."

"Oh. Well, yeah."

She smears some sparkly lip gloss on her lips and takes off her coat. "Why was Ross here anyway?"

I shrug. "He wanted to be taped. Speaking of which, we gotta shoot some more. Come on."

It takes Chelsea a few minutes to get ready and then agree to leave her stuff in the library. Fear of getting chipped, I guess. But Mr. Singer says he'll watch it, so we take off through the mostly empty halls.

"So weird that Ross came to be taped, right?" she asks.

"It's not that weird," I say. "I mean, he does go to this school."

We walk through the halls. It seems most people who are still around really do not want to be filmed.

"This is a violation of privacy!" one boy says. I don't know his name. I don't know anyone's name.

I don't mean to laugh at him, but I can't help it. "No, it's not! You'd be on the video for the big fiftieth-anniversary event."

"Oh. No thanks." He walks away with the group he's with.

"Who was that?" I ask Chelsea.

"Josh Kerms. He's one of those boys who watch the Cartoon Network all day," she says. "I don't know why they are being so weird."

"I know! I mean, it's their school. Wouldn't they want to be a part of it?"

"No, not them." Chelsea looks down at her phone and

then puts it in the front pocket of her blazer. "Kendall and Molly, they're acting all sneaky and weird. They won't tell me where they are."

I almost bring up the Facebook friend request thing, but then I realize it would sound lame to be so excited about friending on Facebook. Instead, I leave Chelsea to her texting and walk a little bit away from her, over to a group of kids hanging out by the vending machine. This video project is actually kind of a good thing for me. It gives me an excuse to just go up to people and be noticed.

The group looks down the hall at Chelsea, who's still texting. What else is new?

"What are you doing?" one of the girls asks me. "Why are you just filming me standing here drinking a soda?"

I laugh. "It's for the fiftieth anniversary. We're trying to get random shots of kids at school."

"God, get people to sign a release form or something!" another girl huffs, and the group walks away.

I look around, trying to find someone else. I didn't think people would respond this way. It's as if everyone expects something horrible to happen. But it's not like we're broadcasting this on the local news or anything.

Chelsea yells from all the way down the hall, "I gotta go. Sorry. Will explain later."

She's going to leave? Just like that? In the middle of our work?

I walk around more, getting some shots of kids playing basketball outside, some girls studying in the hallway, other kids getting extra help.

I even capture a chipping. I don't care that Chelsea says you can't call it that—I can call it what I want to call it. Some girl is walking down the hall, and then another girl just opens her backpack and pours out the crumbs all over her books.

Just like that.

"Oh my God!" the victim yells.

The other girl and her friends laugh and walk away.

"Did you just video that?" the victim asks me.

I nod. "It's for a project, though."

"Well, delete it!" she yells. "I don't want other people to see it! I'll be the girl who got chipped on video."

I don't say anything, and the girl walks closer to me. "This school stinks!" she yells, even louder now. "And that girl you're working with on this dumb video—it's her fault it stinks."

"Chelsea?" I say. It occurs to me that I'm still taping this, and we're basically gossiping about Chelsea behind her back, but I can edit it all out later.

"Yeah, her and her friends. It's their fault. They're the reason we all feel like outsiders," she says, and I realize now is definitely not the time to reveal the fact that I don't know her name. That would surely make her feel even more like an outsider.

"Um . . . hmm," is all I say. "I'll delete the video. Don't worry."

She goes on and on about Chelsea, how she has the perfect life, how everyone loves her. But Chelsea isn't the one who just chipped her. How can this be Chelsea's fault?

And I know the truth—Chelsea doesn't have the perfect life. But I can't just come out and say that.

Is it so cheesy to want a place where all people are included and accepted? I mean, everyone doesn't have to be BFF with everyone else, but at least no one would feel like a loser.

My old school was kind of like that. I suppose it could happen here, too, but it doesn't seem possible at the moment.

It's after five when I walk out to the car to meet my mom. It's freezing and almost pitch-black out because the days are getting shorter. I want to walk around in a sleeping bag to keep warm. My phone makes the twinkling sound to alert me that I have a text message.

> Sorry I had to run out. I'd explain but u wouldn't understand. See u tomorrow.

What does Chelsea think I wouldn't understand? That she

has friends and places to be and exciting things to do? In that case, she's probably right.

The question is, what do Chelsea and those people feel about this place? Do they know they make so many people upset?

The more time I spend with Chelsea, the more I realize she's not that bad. She's actually kind of nice. She bought me Peanut M&M's; she can't be that bad.

The thing is, people just assume things about others, even if they aren't true. I do it all the time. If I ever became friends with Chelsea and her friends, would I automatically make people miserable, too?

And are people ever really aware about how they affect others? Do they know their role here? That's what I need to find out.

14

CHELSEA

Sasha Preston piece of advice: You'll be amazed
at how much you can accomplish when you
don't worry about who gets the credit.

A part of me knows I shouldn't have bailed on Dina, but
when I got a text from Molly saying that it was an emergency
and they needed to talk to me, I had to go call her. It turns
out it wasn't really an emergency; they just needed to ask me
a question about Ross and the note he passed Dina, which I
didn't know anything about anyway. They always jump to the
word "emergency" really fast.

And they refused to tell me where they were, because they
were scared Dina and I would come meet them. They were just at
Starbucks, and it's not like I'd bring Dina to hang out with them.

I was kind of glad to get out of school, though. I felt kind
of weird walking around trying to tape kids I've been in school

with since kindergarten. I never talk to them, so it's weird to just go up to them now. And library boy seems to have disappeared. I have no idea why my mind keeps flopping back to him when I'm in the library, but it does. I wonder if he moved away right after I noticed him. That would be just my luck these days.

My cell phone rings at nine thirty, and I dread answering it because I'm scared who will be on the other line: Dina, mad at me for bailing, or Kendall or Molly, saying something else about Ross that I will feel awkward about. When I look at my phone, I see that it's Dina.

"Hello?" I answer.

"Got her agent!"

"You did?" I guess she's not that mad at me for bailing.

"Yup! I just read about a million articles on Sasha Preston and found her manager's name, and then that led me to her agent."

"Good job," I tell her. I'm only half paying attention because I'm so nervous about everything else that's going on.

"So, we're going to call her agent and tell her that we go to her alma mater middle school and we want to interview her for this project," she says. "I'm sure she'll say yes, because people always want to help kids out. And then we'll figure out when to go meet up with her. Okay?"

"It sounds good to me." I actually mean that, and I'm actually excited about this—which makes me feel even worse about what happened earlier. "Sorry I bailed before," I admit, finally. "Did you get any footage?"

"I did," she says, but she sounds uncertain. Another thing I've never heard from her. "I'm not sure it's right, though. It seems really, like, one-sided, I guess, and boring, which is why I really think we should just focus on the Sasha part, at least for now."

"Oh. Okay." I start to hear yelling coming from downstairs. This always happens at this time of night. It's like my parents' witching hour. I can't stay on the phone with this going on; it's impossible to concentrate. "I gotta go, though. My mom needs to show me something. Bye." I hang up quickly, before Dina can say anything else.

"You're making me look bad. But that's not even the worst part!" I hear my mom scream. I wonder where Alexa is. Sometimes she'll run into my room during their fights. "You're making *yourself* look bad! How can you not even care?"

"You think I don't care?" my dad yells back. He can always yell louder, but my mom says the meaner stuff.

I wish they could just come up with a game plan. Like, if *this* happens, then we'll do *that* instead. It would make things so much easier, and then I'd know they had it all under control. I feel sad for them that things are unraveling. If I could fix everything, I would. But in the meantime, I just want to know that things won't get any worse.

During their fights, I always focus on the most random things. Like the ballerina figurine I got for my eighth birthday. Kendall found it in some fancy shop on Cape Cod. Her grandparents used to have a summer home there.

My cell phone starts ringing, and I answer it without looking who it is first. It's probably Dina calling again to complain since I basically cut her off twice in one day.

"Chelsea." No, it's Molly. Even the way she says people's names sounds mean, even when they're supposed to be her best friends. "I need to talk to you."

"Yeah?" I put a million pillows up against my door and lean back on them, hoping that the pillows will block out the sound of my parents' screaming. "Is this about Ross again? I know he spent, like, two minutes with Dina for the video. It's not that big of a deal."

"It's not about that," she says, and then she's quiet for a really long time. "It's about your dad."

My heart starts pounding. Real, heavy pounding, like the bass at the loudest rock concert you've ever been to. And when I look down at my chest, I can see it thumping, almost popping out from my skin.

I've never felt this intense panic before. All I want is for the world to stop. I want to hang up and pretend she never said anything.

"What?" my voice comes out like a whisper. I can't believe we're having this discussion. Me and Molly. Molly with the four-car garage and the pool and the tennis court and the Burberry coat for each season. Mean Molly. Of course she'd be the one to find out and bring this up.

"We know. We all know."

If life were a TV show like *Sasha Says So*, she'd ask me how was I doing, how my whole family was doing. She'd come over with pints of ice cream, and we'd sit and talk and she'd be a nice friend.

"You do?"

"Yes. And we can't believe it. We also can't believe you kept it from us for so long. My parents knew this whole time, and I overheard them talking. It was so easy, almost too easy. Did you really think you'd keep it from us forever?"

But this isn't a TV show. This is the part where I lose all my friends because I can't get the newest jeans, because I don't get a car when I turn sixteen, because my parents can't afford to go to Riverbay on Saturday nights.

"How come you didn't tell us?" she asks. But the thing is, her voice doesn't have a tone of concern; it has a tone of annoyance, like she's mad because she didn't hear the latest gossip. She sounded the exact same way when Lance Friedrich broke up with Hope Allen and no one told her.

"Well, I was hoping it would pass." I don't even know what I'm saying anymore. I literally have no control over the words that are coming out of my mouth.

"What would pass? Like it was just a phase or something? And he'd get his job back?" Now her tone isn't so much annoyed as condescending. Molly can go from annoyed to condescending in about ten seconds flat.

"It's a really hard thing." That's all I can manage to say, and it's nothing at all. I'm wasting the rest of my brainpower trying to figure out how I can get off the phone.

"You should have told us."

This isn't *Sasha Says So,* because she doesn't say things like, *I'm sure it's so hard* or *I can't even imagine* or *We're here for you.*

Those things would be condescending, too, but they're the kinds of things you're supposed to say.

"I'm sorry. I just couldn't. I'm still having trouble processing it myself."

"Uh-huh," she mutters.

Molly is actually mad that I didn't tell her about this. It's so obvious that she doesn't care at all about me, she just cares about herself.

"Well, everyone's gonna know eventually, just like we found out," she says. "And as your friend, I felt like you should know that." She pauses. "Aren't you worried that our friends know? Soon everyone at school will know."

She sneezes, and I don't say "Bless you."

"I guess."

"Why are you, like, dead right now, Chelsea?" she asks. "You're, like, speaking in this zombie tone. I can't even tell how you feel."

"Molly, I have to go."

"No, don't get off the phone with me, Chelsea." She drags out the last syllable of my name. I've always hated when she does that, but I hate it even more right now. "We've been friends since forever. You can't just run away. I need to know if you're friends with that new girl now. Is she your BFF? Is that why you didn't tell us? Because you were so busy telling her all about your problems?"

"Molly, I have to go," I repeat. It feels like my whole room is spinning. The pastel spirals on the wallpaper rotate around each other like I'm in some kind of special, wacky room at the amusement park. The darker pink threads of my carpet look like they're sticking up and growing taller and taller above the other pale pink threads.

"Fine, bye," she says. "I thought you'd at least thank me for preparing you for tomorrow."

I hang up without saying good-bye.

15

DINA

Video tip: A transition can really help bring together two moments, but don't overuse transitions, because they can also be distracting.

Chelsea and I are in the library after school. I'm looking through old yearbooks again, trying not to bother Chelsea. She's been weird all day, barely talking to me during social studies when we were supposed to be working on our project. She kept looking to the back of the room at her stupid friends Kendall and Molly and the rest of them. Kendall and Molly are the only ones I know because they're the main ones. The rest are stragglers. And besides, they all sound and look exactly the same to me.

I shouldn't say they're stupid. They're not.

It's pathetic but true. Even with all their meanness, they seem to have fun here. That's really all I'm looking for.

I close the yearbook I've been looking at, and I wonder if this is the time for me to bring up the thing about her dad. "Are you okay?" I ask finally.

Chelsea lowers her eyes. "You've asked me that a million times. Stop."

I nod. Guess it's not the time. I open up one of the library laptops and find the info on Sasha Preston's agent again. "Okay, here's the number. Her agent is this person Charlotte Weingarten, at International Talent Management and Associates." I point at the computer screen.

"Okay."

"I'm calling her."

"You are?"

I'm not sure how she thought I'd get in touch with her. Smoke signals?

"Don't you think you should try e-mail?" Chelsea asks.

Oh, yeah. E-mail. "No. My e-mail address is supergirl922@hotmail.com. She won't take me seriously."

Chelsea laughs. It bursts out like she hasn't laughed in a million years.

"Good point," she says. "Okay, call."

I take out my cell phone. "Is Mr. Singer gonna get mad? Are we allowed to use cell phones in the library?"

Chelsea shrugs. "It's fine. Just talk quietly."

I dial and the phone rings three times, and when a voice answers, I say, "Hi, may I speak to Charlotte Weingarten, please?" in my most adult-sounding voice.

"May I ask who's calling?" the voice on the other end of the phone asks me.

"Yes, my name is Dina Gross. I'm inquiring about a project for Ms. Sasha Preston."

Chelsea pats me on the arm and opens her eyes really wide. She thinks I'm doing a good job.

"Please hold."

International Talent Management and Associates has this very intense-sounding voice on their hold button, going on and on about the kinds of services they offer their clients. *The finest in talent management and promotion. We've been a leader in this field for over fifty years, enabling the most successful talents to reach the highest levels of success.*

Finally, the voice stops and I hear, "Charlotte Wein-garten."

"Oh, hello, Ms. Weingarten," I say. "My name is Dina Gross. And I'm hoping you can help me. I have a very exciting project for Sasha Preston."

"What is it?" This Charlotte Weingarten lady's voice is harsh and aggressive, and I start to feel a little less confident.

"It's a video, I mean, um, a documentary." Chelsea kicks

me and makes a face like I'm totally lying to this person. But I'm not. I just used the word "documentary" to make it sound more important and official.

"I'm not sure how Sasha Preston fits into a documentary. Is this about the controversial fire in the studio from a few years back? Because seriously, move on."

A controversial fire seems intriguing, but I don't have time to wonder about it now. "It's actually about her hometown. Her middle school, specifically."

There's a pause on the other end of the line, and I wonder if I should repeat myself. At that same second, I see Mr. Singer coming toward the back of the library with one of the blue carts overflowing with books to be shelved. I put the phone between my ear and my shoulder and tilt my head, hoping Mr. Singer doesn't see it.

"She doesn't have time for nonsense like that," Charlotte says finally.

"What? No, I mean, it's not nonsense. See, my, um, friend and I are working on this video for the fiftieth anniversary of our school, and she went here, and we thought it would be interesting to have her take—"

Ms. Weingarten interrupts me. "I am running a business here. If you're in some kind of silly fan club, please just visit her site."

"No, it's not a fan club." I laugh because saw a bunch of Sasha Preston fan sites in my research and they were so cheesy. Then I remember who I'm on the phone with and swallow. "Please just give her my number. I'd like to discuss it with her."

"I'm not sure who this is, but I'm beginning to think this is some sort of joke. And I do *not* have time for jokes."

I ask again if I can give her my number and if she can pass it to Sasha. She says yes, but I can't be sure she actually writes it down.

After the call ends, all I can really focus on is how I just called Chelsea my friend on the phone to Sasha's agent. I wonder if she's mad that I said that, because it's pretty hard to tell if she's actually my friend or not.

And I'm annoyed at myself for focusing on this seemingly trivial but yet not at all trivial thing after a very important phone call.

Chelsea looks at me and says, "You're hilarious."

"I am?"

"Yeah, and the funniest part is, you don't even realize it."

So maybe she's not annoyed? Maybe we are friends.

"Well, I doubt that's gonna work." I roll my head from side to side trying to get my neck to stop aching. "We're just going to have to go into the city and find her on our own."

"What?"

"Sure. Next time she writes on Twitter where she is, we'll hop on the train and go."

I open Sasha's eighth-grade yearbook again and look at the photos for the millionth time. I have to find her. I have to prove that I can do something cool, and make a good video, and actually accomplish something at this school.

"Look at this message this girl Eleanor wrote: *Million Cup Masquerade, 4-ever.* What does that even mean?" I ask Chelsea.

"No clue." She points to the next page. "Look at this one: *Never forget Ladybug and the tags.*"

"So weird!"

"I guess we could go try to get some more footage," Chelsea says. "These yearbook jokes are funny, but we can't use them for the project, and we can't just wait on this Sasha thing to happen. We'll end up with nothing."

I'm kind of shocked Chelsea just suggested that, but I try to act calm.

We're walking down the hall when we see all of Chelsea's friends. All together, laughing and smiling and having the best time ever. They look like the characters on *Sasha Says So*, the ones who are always in the background in the hallway, making it look like there are more than three people at the school.

Did she know they were all hanging out without her?

They stop walking. Then we stop walking, and Chelsea goes over to talk to them. I stay back a little.

Their conversation goes on longer than I expect. Luckily, we're near the main office, so I sit down on one of the benches in the hallway.

After a while, I feel like a total idiot. How long is she going to talk to them? We're supposed to be videoing people—it was her suggestion! And now I'm sitting here all by myself. It's always worse to sit by yourself when other people can see you. If people can't see you by yourself, it's really not so bad. It's kind of like that whole if-a-tree-falls-in-the-forest-can-anyone-hear-it thing. If you're sitting by yourself and no one sees you, are you really alone?

I don't understand why Chelsea can say that I'm hilarious and laugh at what I say and be impressed with how I talked to Sasha Preston's agent, but I'm not good enough to be an actual friend.

I didn't expect it to be this hard.

I don't know what it takes to get into their group. What am I doing wrong?

Sure, I don't have those fancy jeans. Not yet, anyway. But I'm getting them. I just need to work on my mom a little more.

But is it only the jeans? I mean, my hair is pretty shiny, like theirs. I look okay, and I even have my pretty days.

She's still talking. It's been five minutes already.

I watch her down the hallway, the way she stands, leaning all of her weight on her right leg. Her jeans are tucked into her tall leather riding boots perfectly, without any gaping or bulging. Her long cardigan sweater hits the back of her legs at the perfect spot, like it was made for her.

Yeah, I can see why everyone thinks Chelsea Stern has the perfect life. It certainly looks perfect.

But I know the truth.

Once she knows that I know, she'll be my friend. Not in a blackmail kind of way. In an *I understand* kind of way.

"Sorry," she says, walking over to me. She looks sweaty and her hair is flat, like she's been pushing it down over and over again.

"What was that about?" I ask.

"Huh? What do you mean?"

"It seemed like something serious was going on."

"Oh, no." She shrugs. "Nothing really."

She's lying. Again. I can tell.

16

CHELSEA

Sasha Preston piece of advice: Shower at night.
It makes your life and your mornings much easier.

After I get out of the shower that night, I see five texts
from Kendall.

> chelsea - where r u

> why r u ignoring me?

> seriously - so rude, call me NOW.

And more like that. I call her right away.

"Why are you ignoring my texts now?" Kendall asks.

I'm in my bathroom with my face pressed against the cold
pink tile of the wall. I don't know if I've ever been this nervous.
Molly says what's on her mind even if it's mean, but Kendall

makes me nervous because she always seems like she's up to something—a trick-up-her-sleeve kind of person. I can never tell what she's thinking.

"In the shower."

"Don't kill me, okay?"

"What are you talking about?" I'm sweating now, cold sweats that start at my forehead.

"Some more people—like, besides us—may know about your dad."

"Who are 'some people'?"

I hear Kendall chewing gum. It sounds more obnoxious than ever before, and it always sounds obnoxious. "Marcus . . . Eric . . ." She pauses. "Ross. They're your best friends, too. I didn't feel right keeping it from them."

Ross knows. Even Ross knows.

"You told me in the hallway today that you'd keep it between us and the other girls," I say. I'm a perfect combination of angry and sad right now. If I were a cartoon character, I'd have fire coming out of my ears and tears streaming down my cheeks. "Remember? What changed since then?"

"I just couldn't keep it between us. So don't hate me. It's probably better it's out in the open." She stops talking but keeps chewing. "My mom's on the phone with your mom right now. She feels really bad."

"You weren't supposed to tell your mom that you all know now. Molly said she wasn't telling hers," I say. "I don't want my parents to know that all of the kids know. They'll feel even worse."

"They were going to find out, Chelsea. Why are you so concerned with protecting your parents? They're grown-ups."

I don't respond to that. She obviously doesn't understand any of what I'm going through.

Life will never be the same again, or even close to the same again, not tonight, not ever again. I need to run away somewhere. I'm totally going to end up with no friends. I'm going to end up exactly like Dina, but I'm not confident enough to handle it as well as she does.

My mom calls me down for dinner, so I guess she's off the phone with Kendall's mom. I hang up with Kendall and head downstairs. Oh, joy, this is going to be fabulous.

"Who's this girl you're working with on the project?" my mom asks me as she's getting dinner ready, and by that I mean putting the Chinese food on platters so we're not eating out of the plastic containers. She doesn't even notice that I decided to shower before dinner.

"This girl Dina. She's new."

"Gwen said you have been spending afternoons working with her in the library."

"Uh-huh. It's a project, Mom. We have to work on it. Molly and Kendall didn't save me a spot in their project group. Remember?" I pour myself some seltzer and sit down. I don't feel like setting the table, and I hope my mom doesn't ask me to. "And you haven't wondered where I've been all these afternoons after school?"

"I figured you were out with the girls." She turns around, leans back against the granite counter, and looks at me. "I hoped that's where you were."

"Sorry to disappoint."

"Chelsea, please lose the attitude. How many times do I have to ask you to talk to me with some respect?" She brings the chicken and broccoli over to the table. "Things are hard enough."

"I know. Fine. Sorry."

"Shhh," my mom says, even though I haven't even said anything, really. Then I see my dad walking into the kitchen. Today is a new record; it's almost seven and he's still in his workout clothes.

We eat our Chinese food, and Alexa talks to us about the science project they have to do where they collect bugs and save them on Styrofoam. She doesn't even seem grossed out by it. Alexa isn't as girly as I am, I guess.

My mom seems to be really interested. Like *too*

interested. She smiles too much, and it's all so fake that I can barely stand it. My dad doesn't say anything. He eats his moo shu chicken and then clears his plate and goes back into the den.

He doesn't even look at his BlackBerry anymore.

Finally, the pain of dinner ends, and I go up to my room to study for my English test. It's on the Shakespeare play *The Tempest*. I wish I could be in Miranda's shoes; at least she doesn't have to worry about her dad having a job.

I can barely focus on studying with my parents downstairs. They're not fighting now, just talking loudly, and I alternate between wanting to hear what they're saying and not wanting to hear what they're saying.

I'm writing a practice essay on the symbolism of magic in the play when I get a text. It's from Ross.

R u OK?

This is insanity. Ross is asking me if I'm okay. Ross who has a Mercedes, a BMW, and a Bentley. Ross has a live-in cook and a live-in housekeeper and the longest driveway on Long Island. No joke. It's been in books and everything. The last thing I need is for Ross to know.

"Yes, I'm okay," I say as soon as Ross answers the phone. "Do you really care if I'm okay?"

"Chel-seagull, I've known you since kindergarten. Of course I care."

It is kind of cute when he calls me Chel-seagull.

"Whatever, Ross. I don't want to talk about it with you." That's what I say, but the truth is, Ross is actually easier to talk to than my girlfriends. Ross doesn't gossip like they do or make you feel bad when you don't have the newest stuff. I kind of do want to talk about it with him, but for some reason I can't admit that. And if I do talk to him about this stuff, will he still even like me?

"Fine. We'll talk about other stuff. Did Molly get a nose job?"

I laugh. Is he for real? Or is he just trying to make me laugh?

"Yeah, last summer. You just realized this now? Grunny, it's November." While I'm talking to him, I open up Google and try to find out more about Sasha Preston and her rude agent. At least it's something else to focus on.

"It looks bad. She should have gone to Dr. Fitzsimmons."

"You're disgusting."

"Why? You know I'm right."

"Yeah. It does look bad." I don't care that I'm being gossipy. I don't care that I'm spending my time discussing nose jobs. Sometimes, when things are bad, you just can't be as good as you normally try to be.

"So, what about you and that new girl?" he asks.

"Huh?" I can't believe people are still bringing this up with me.

"Are you guys tight?" Ross asks.

"We're just working on a project together."

"Oh. Okay. Calm down, Seagull. I'm just asking."

"I gotta go, Ross. Thanks for checking in."

After we're off the phone, I keep going over the conversation in my head. He was nice to check in on me, but he didn't really say much. And he asked about Dina.

But I don't know why I even care. It's not as though he likes Dina. He likes me. That's what everyone says.

Right?

DINA

Video tip: Fading in and out of black is a
good way to show that time has passed.

"Do you know Ross Grunner?" Chelsea asks me after
school. We're at our usual table in the library.

I don't know why she's asking me this. There are so many
other things we should be discussing. On the top of the list
is her secret. Lately, all I can think about is the fact that she
has a secret, a big secret, and I'm waiting anxiously for her to
tell me about it.

I nod. "Yeah, he was in our video, remember? And I'd
know him anyway. Isn't he, like, the king of Rockwood Hills?"

She laughs. "I know what you mean." And then she just
keeps laughing, and I'm not sure why. It wasn't that funny.

She turns around and watches some kid push a cart of
library books like it's the most interesting thing in the world.

I go on with the conversation. "I also know who he is because I listen to Maura go on and on about Ross Grunner every single day at lunch." I probably shouldn't bad-mouth someone at my lunch table, but, oh well, too late.

"Ross Grunner doesn't like Maura Eastly, so she can get over him really fast. Ross and his friends think she's one of the ugliest girls in the grade."

"That's horrible. Why do you guys discuss that?"

"I don't know. We just do. Eric is always keeping a rank of the girls in the grade."

That's so mean—but also kind of intriguing. I wonder if I've been here long enough to be on the list. "Why'd you want to know if I know him?"

"Just curious." Chelsea puts her feet up on the chair across from her.

For some reason I don't believe her, but I don't press it further. It seems like Chelsea keeps a lot of secrets—about her dad, what her friends talk about, and now this.

How can we ever be real friends if she keeps this many secrets? Though I'm not sure we'll ever be real friends. Not at the rate we're going.

"So, found out more stuff about Sasha?" Chelsea asks. She's looking at her phone as she talks to me.

"I did. She's shooting a movie in New York this weekend."

Chelsea finally looks up. "She is?"

"Yes, and we're going."

I don't know what is bringing on this boldness. It could be that I really want to meet Sasha and ask her what she thinks about Rockwood Hills Middle School. It could be that I really want to hang out with Chelsea outside of school. That's what will determine if we're real friends or just two people working on a project together. Or maybe I just want to do something crazy. Something the old Dina would've done.

Either way, I really wonder if my parents will let me go into Manhattan by myself. I'm very curious to find that out.

"This weekend? I'm not sure."

"We have to get this done, Chelsea." My words come out with attitude; even I can hear it.

"You're right. Whatever. I don't need to go dress shopping with Kendall. I don't care if she gets a new dress for Cami's bat mitzvah. Just because it's at the Ritz-Carlton doesn't mean that everyone has to get a new dress. It's so stupid."

It's like Chelsea doesn't realize what she's saying as she's talking, and then when she stops, she can hear herself and gets embarrassed.

"Yeah, I'm not getting a new dress. I'm not even invited," I say, mostly under my breath because I don't want to be one of those people that others feel bad for.

Chelsea's looking at her phone again. When she looks up, I can see she's crying.

I don't know what to do. "Are you okay?" I ask.

"I'm fine. I'm just sick of everyone."

I reach to put my arm around her shoulder, and then I pull it away. I don't think we're that kind of close yet. And maybe she's referring to being sick of me—what do I know?

"We'll go find Sasha this weekend. It will totally make things better." I smile. "For both of us."

She shrugs and keeps wiping her eyes.

"Are you allowed to go into the city by yourself?" I ask. I hope this doesn't make me sound like the biggest baby and loser in the entire world, but I just got here. I don't know what people are and aren't allowed to do. I don't even know what I'm allowed to do!

"Yeah. I do it all the time." She makes a snotty face. "Are you?"

"Oh, yeah. I mean, I've been in the city a million times. We used to come in from Massachusetts, like, every other weekend."

"Really?" She squishes her eyes together.

"No." I laugh. "I just wanted to see if you were paying attention."

She laughs and shakes her head like I'm totally crazy. I

don't even know what I'm saying anymore, but I can't worry about it now.

She puts her head down on the library table and whines, "Ugh, everything is just so annoying. It was easier when I was stuck at home with mono!"

I've been meaning to ask her this since I met her, but the time never seemed right. Now I have to. "I don't get it. Do you like it here or not? Everyone thinks you've got the best life ever and you live for this school. But from what you say, it doesn't seem that great."

She sits up and folds her arms across her chest. "Everyone thinks I have the best life ever?"

I nod. The way she's staring at me, I feel like I shouldn't have brought this up, but it's too late now.

"Who's 'everyone'?"

"I don't know. Mostly the three people I talk to: Maura, Katherine, and Trisha."

"They don't know what they're talking about."

I lean back. "Come on, Chelsea. You know you're popular. The most popular girl in the grade." I pause and notice her confused expression. "You know that, right?"

"You sound like some kind of cheesy video that they make us watch in health class." She takes her phone out of her pocket. "I gotta go. E-mail me the plans for finding Sasha Preston."

"You'll see how awesome it's going to be," I tell her. And I really, really hope I'm right about this one. This feels like my ultimate test, and I need to pass.

The next few days fly by because I'm so excited about going into the city with Chelsea.

But I'm also thinking about Ross Grunner and his friends' ranking of the girls in our grade. Where would I be on that list? I wonder.

My mind always seems to go back to Ross—even when I was thinking about something totally different just a minute before. The little groups of freckles on his face are so cute, and every day when we're in social studies, I wonder if he's going to pass me a note again.

Maybe focusing on him is a good thing, because it's keeping my mind off the fact that my parents don't know I'm going into Manhattan. They think a girl from my grade invited me over for the day. I made up a name for the girl—Fiona Baker. That way, just in case they try to find her number, they won't be able to and they'll call my cell. The last thing I need is them calling a girl's house.

I didn't mean to lie to them, but I couldn't risk them saying no to this plan.

I'm not the kind of girl who lies to her parents.

Rockwood Hills is so messed up. I can tell it's changed me. But it's my parents' fault. They're the ones who made us move here.

From my Internet research I learned that Sasha Preston is shooting her first movie. It's called *Reckless Abandon*, and it's about a girl in her thirties and her younger sister who leave their fancy New York City lifestyle to travel cross-country and change their lives.

It sounds like something my mom would love. And it's cool that Sasha can do TV and movies at the same time. More people will know about her when she's in movies, not just the kids who watch *Sasha Says So*.

They're shooting today in SoHo, where the girls live at the beginning of the movie. SoHo stands for "South of Houston." Houston is a street in downtown Manhattan, and they pronounce it "House-ton," not "Hugh-ston." I had to look up where the neighborhood is because I didn't want to have to ask Chelsea about everything.

"We need to take the C or the E subway to Spring Street," I tell her as we're getting off the Long Island Rail Road at Penn Station, this huge train station right in the middle of Manhattan. Tons of trains and subways all come through here. It's really confusing, but I try to follow the signs for the subway.

"For a girl who's not even from here, you really know a lot about the city," Chelsea says. "I never know where I am. We always take cabs. Well, I mean, we used to. I don't know what I'm saying."

I know what she's saying, but I don't tell her that. Still, I wonder how long she's going to keep dropping hints about her dad losing his job before she just tells me.

Or how long I can go without spilling the beans.

Keeping secrets is really not my specialty. I'm kind of impressed that I've gone this long.

As we're walking through Penn Station, I spot Kendall and all those girls with a group of ladies, probably their moms.

Kendall is really easy to spot. She has a bright red Burberry coat even though all the other girls have black. Plus her hair is the color of lemonade. It almost looks fluorescent, but in a good way.

Chelsea's walking really fast and I don't think she notices them. She would know if they were coming into the city today, wouldn't she? Is it possible that she chose hanging out with me over them?

I decide not to say anything. I already feel messy enough with my hair in a ponytail instead of blown out like theirs. And my green poncho is like a dirty dish towel next to their beautiful raincoats.

As much as I want all of them to see me with Chelsea so they can see that I really am a viable addition to the group, I don't think this is the right time.

We buy MetroCards at the touch-screen machine and walk down the stairs to the C and E platform.

I'm going on and on about what it'll be like to see Sasha and how much I hope we get to talk to her, and how long we should wait if people try to kick us out and all this stuff. I know I'm talking too much. But I'm so excited that I can't help it.

"So we'll say we're doing a report for school," I tell Chelsea. "People won't say no to that, right?"

Chelsea pops a piece of gum in her mouth. It smells fruity and delicious. "A report on Sasha Preston? She's not, like, Audrey Hepburn. I mean, she's famous but she's not really report-worthy yet. Is she?"

"No, we'll say we're doing a report on movie shoots. We're taking a film-studies class." I clap my hands—I'm so proud of my white lie. But I'm also a little scared at how good I'm getting at lying.

"Yeah, right. A film-studies class in middle school?" Chelsea scoffs. "Like that would ever happen."

"We had one in my old school, actually." I pause and wonder if I should e-mail Mr. Doylen, the teacher. Maybe we could have a class like that at Rockwood Hills one day. "We'll say we go to another school. We'll make something up." I lean back against one of the pillars.

"Chelsea?" we hear someone say. We both look up at the same time. It's Kendall, and all the other girls and their moms are behind her. "Are you going to the trunk show?"

Kendall looks at me and barely smiles. She doesn't say hi.

I hope she doesn't think I'm stealing her friend. We can all be friends. I sound like a cheesy children's show, but sometimes those characters, even though they're usually in bizarre animal costumes, have the right ideas about life.

"No . . . um . . . I decided not to," Chelsea says. After an awkward moment, all the other girls rush up to hug her like it's been years since they've seen each other. The moms go on and on about how pretty her hair looks and how her coat looks brand-new and all these things that seem to be so weird for moms to get so excited about.

And then they all ask her about her mother, and where she is, and what she's doing.

The moms don't even look at me. They don't notice me. Or maybe they do but they don't realize that I'm with Chelsea.

I don't know if I should introduce myself or not.

It's not like their daughters are even saying hi to me.

"So what are you doing in the city today?" Molly asks. Her hair is blown straight, too, and her lips are extra glossy.

"Working on the thing for school," Chelsea says, and looks down the platform to see if the train is coming. "Actually, I should really be in the front of the subway for where I'm going, so I gotta go."

She walks away and doesn't make sure that I'm behind her or with her or anything. I follow along, though, because why would I stand here by myself?

"They never take the subway. They were following me," Chelsea says when we get to the other end of the platform.

"That's kind of psychotic." And what I mean is that Chelsea is kind of psychotic if she thinks that. Plus I'm still annoyed that she didn't even acknowledge that I was doing the project with her. She didn't even acknowledge that I was standing with her.

"I know. They are psychotic."

She doesn't even get what I'm saying.

Right then, I'm tempted to go home. I lied to my parents, and I feel bad about that. And all the lying isn't even worth it, because Chelsea doesn't even care about the project, or care that I'm here, or care about anything.

Finally, the C train pulls into the station and we get on. Chelsea sits down, and I sit across from her.

I don't understand how the people here have the power to make me feel so bad about myself. I feel like life should be getting better. But it just doesn't seem that way.

18

CHELSEA

Sasha Preston piece of advice: People are happier when they're wearing comfortable shoes, especially when walking around all day.

I am the psychotic one.

I'm the one who can't get a handle on things, who decides to be nice to Dina one minute and then completely ignore her the next.

It's just that I couldn't introduce her to all the moms, because they wouldn't get it. They'd think I abandoned their daughters, just like my mom has abandoned them, even though that's totally not the case. Really, it's their daughters who are abandoning me, and they're the ones who are abandoning my mom.

We get off the train at Spring Street, and I'm happy it has stopped raining, since we have to walk a few blocks to where Dina thinks the shoot is taking place. I really have no idea how she found out all of this information. I think they generally like to keep these things pretty secretive.

Dina has a way of finding things out, and it kind of scares me when I think about it too much.

There are silver trailers parked all around Spring Street and lots of trucks and lights and all these people wearing headsets that make the set seem totally official and important. Some people are gathered around on the corner trying to get glimpses of the actors and actresses.

I don't think they're all here for Sasha Preston. Ben Affleck is in this movie, too, and he's a big deal. I think he's the guy Sasha's older sister ends up marrying. They meet on a farm in Montana or something. Once Dina said we were coming to the set, I just couldn't help researching the movie a little bit.

"Where is she?" I ask. I expect Dina to know, but how can she? All I know right now is that I've gone from depressed to excited in less than ten seconds. I've pretty much stopped thinking about Kendall and Molly and their moms, and I'm not thinking about things at home, either.

Being near a movie shoot is exciting—it's impossible to focus on anything else. And I want to tell Dina how grateful I am that she found out about this and dragged us here, but I can't figure out a way to say that without seeming really weird.

Dina's phone starts ringing. She has her ringtone set to "Here Comes the Sun" by the Beatles. That's my dad's favorite song, but I don't know any kids our age who really listen to it.

"Be quiet, okay? My parents don't know I'm here," she says before she picks up.

I'll be quiet, but I don't think she realizes that we're standing on a city street with people talking and horns blaring and all this noise. Me being quiet probably won't make such a difference.

"Hello?" she says.

She doesn't say anything else for a few minutes, and I start to get nervous. I didn't realize she hadn't told her parents where she was going. I wish she had told me about this sooner, because I told my parents I was going into the city with her, since I wouldn't have been allowed to go in all alone. My parents don't know her parents, but you never know what could happen—they might call just to say hello. Or they could run into them randomly and be introduced, and then they'd know who they are. In a small, gossipy town like Rockwood Hills, anything could happen.

"I told you. I'm with Fiona."

Fiona? I don't think there's a Fiona in our grade. I don't think there's a Fiona in our school.

"Where are *you*?" She laughs, still on the phone. "What? I can't hear you. Dad, you're breaking up. I'll call you later." She hits End and puts the phone back in her pocket.

"What was that all about?" I ask her.

"Oh, you know, just parent stuff."

I can tell she doesn't want to talk about it, so I let it go because I, of all people, understand not wanting to talk about something.

"Come on, let's walk over to Wooster. I have a feeling we'll be able to see more from there," Dina says, and I follow along. There's something about Dina that makes you trust her, or at least *want* to trust her. It's like she's older or wiser or something, or maybe she just does good research.

It takes us a few minutes to break through the crowds on the sidewalks, but we do, and when we get onto Wooster, we get a pretty good spot. I think we're close to where we need to be, because I see even more bright lights and sound equipment.

"What do we do now?" I ask Dina.

"We wait," she says.

It starts raining again, and after a few minutes I can't take it anymore. I'm antsy to get this whole meeting-Sasha-thing started, and on top of that I'm anxious and upset about Kendall and Molly being in the city with their moms without me. I don't know which is worse.

"So what's our plan?" I ask Dina. I sound like a little kid, especially because I just asked her basically the same thing a few minutes ago. "What are we going to say to her?"

"Well, we should say first thing that we go to Rockwood Hills. That'll give her a reason to talk to us." Dina's so confident about this, like she's done it before, like nothing ever fazes her. I swear she'd probably walk right up to the White House and ring the bell.

"There she is!" I yell, and all these people turn around and stare at me like I'm some kind of crazy stalker. It's Dina who is the stalker, who found Sasha and then got us here—and it's actually pretty cool.

Sasha's coming out of her trailer wearing a slinky red dress and skinny heels. It looks so funny because it's raining. People are holding umbrellas for her as she walks.

"Let's move closer," Dina says.

We push our way through the crowds and get as close as we can to Sasha and the street with stores and apartment buildings that make up the main set. This is one of those moments that's big and amazing, and I have a feeling I will want to replay it in my head over and over again when I get home.

Dina bends down and reaches into her backpack, kind of making a scene, taking things out and putting things back in. I wonder if people are going to think we're a security risk.

"The yearbook!" I yelp as soon as I see it, drawing even more attention to ourselves.

Dina nods. "Yup, we can hold it up! She'll be totally intrigued. Don't you think?"

I nod. I want to hug her for thinking of the yearbook at the perfect time. It's almost like this is too easy, because there's a minute when Sasha is just standing there waving to fans, like she's happy we're all here. And it's so weird to think that she's really only four years older than me, and she has a TV show and now she's going to be in a movie. When she went to Rockwood Hills, her life was probably similar to mine. I mean, similar before everything got messed up. But now it's totally different.

"Sasha Preston!" Dina yells. "Sasha Preston! We go to your old school! Rockwood Hills Middle School!"

Now the rest of the people are really starting to seem annoyed, looking at us like we're dumb kids, but the thing is, Sasha's kind of a kid, too. And we're not dumb kids; we're here for a project. It's not like these people are supposed to be here, either; they're loitering on a movie set, just like we are.

Dina stands on her tiptoes. "We have your old yearbook!"

Everyone's facial expressions change after she says that, and they all turn to look at Dina and whisper to one another. I wonder if the yearbook is worth a lot of money. I hope someone doesn't try to steal it and put it on eBay.

Sasha still hasn't really turned around.

"Sasha!" Dina yells again.

Uh-oh. I don't think this is working. I can't tell if Sasha hears us or not, because she's just looking out into the crowd. And then a minute later, she's walking away with the umbrella holders. She's walking past the trailers, over to a totally separate area.

"See, that's another amazing thing about movies and movie sets—like there weren't already a million amazing things," Dina says. "The whole craft services thing, oh my God. They have to constantly provide snacks and treats and meals to everyone who's working on the movie. It's, like, the best food ever. Come to think of it, I'm hungry. We should go over there to find Sasha and to get some food, too!"

"Um, that'd be psycho," I say. I don't want to admit this to Dina, but I'm getting more and more soaked as we stand out here, and I think it's ruining my mood. Even though I was excited and happy before, it seems to be fading now. And if we actually do get to talk to Sasha, I'll probably be too scared to even open my mouth. There has to be an easier way to make a good video. "Besides, calling out to her didn't work."

"Don't worry," Dina says. "We got here. We'll make this happen."

For some stupid reason, I believe her. That's so Dina— making things happen. I wish I could be like that, instead of just dwelling on all the bad stuff.

A few minutes later, the crowd breaks a bit and we get to move closer to the set. There's a group of people walking back and forth on the sidewalk, but they're being guided. They keep stopping and then starting, walking the same stretch of sidewalk over and over again. It's all lit up with these huge silver lights.

"The extras!" Dina exclaims, again, calling too much attention to ourselves. "That's what we'll do. That's our way to get to Sasha."

"Huh?" It's raining harder now, and I pull up my hood.

"Come on. Follow me," Dina says. And I realize that even though she's new and I'm usually in charge, I kind of follow her around a lot. Isn't it supposed to be the other way around?

Right when the guys with the headsets are turned away for a second, we sneak onto that really lit-up stretch of sidewalk. We join the group of people walking back and forth and start walking with them.

"What are we doing?" I tug on Dina's raincoat sleeve. "I feel really, really weird. Can we just go?"

"We're pretending we're extras," she whispers. "Okay? Just act natural. Go with the flow. Thank God for your Burberry coat; we fit right in."

"Glad I could help," I say. "But Sasha doesn't even seem to be in this scene. How is this getting us closer to her?"

"Just wait. It's better than standing out in the crowd."

We walk back and forth for at least fifteen minutes, and nothing happens at all. It's really boring being an extra, because all we're doing is walking on a sidewalk and they keep making us do it over and over again. I can't even tell if they're shooting us, because nobody looks over to what we're doing.

"Why haven't you girls been to makeup?" someone yells.

We look around.

"You two. You haven't been to makeup. We're going to need to do this scene all over again."

"Oh, um." Dina throws up her hands. "Yeah, I guess we got shuffled away from there."

What is she talking about? Is she out of her mind?

"Okay, go on, go on." The guy shakes his head. He's tall and super skinny, wearing all black, and he keeps fiddling with his headset. "Go that way, ask for Julian, and be back here ASAP."

"Will do!" Dina yells, and grabs my hand.

"Do you know where we're supposed to go?" I talk through my teeth.

"No idea. But we don't want them to find out we're not extras," she says. "And besides, we have more important work to do."

I nod. I can't exactly just run away right now, so I'm pretty much stuck doing whatever Dina says.

"Okay, look around and see if there are any headset guys," she whispers. "I'll keep an eye out for Sasha."

I look around. I'm not sure why she's whispering right now. She really doesn't need to, since there's really no one around this corner of the set. But it's better than her yelping, which made everyone stare at us.

"No headset guys that I can see," I tell her.

"Okay. Just follow me. Don't do anything crazy."

I can't believe she says that, like I'm the one who does crazy stuff. That would be her!

We walk toward the food and Dina tries to sneak a croissant, but I slap her hand just in time. Someone is totally going to see her doing that!

And then I realize we're standing only a few feet away from Sasha.

At this moment in time, it feels like everything else in the world has stopped. Dina's frozen right in front of me. I have no idea what will happen from here, but for some reason it's the best I've felt in forever, since before the summer, before the mono, since everything with my dad.

I can't tell if Dina's talking to me or talking out loud to herself when she says, "Yes, I've lied to my parents, snuck onto a movie set as an extra, and now I'm stalking Sasha Preston while she's trying to eat."

Then the next thing I know, Dina's tapping Sasha on the shoulder.

Dina is tapping Sasha on her shoulder! Dina's smiling, like she's about to laugh and I feel like I'm about to laugh, too, from giddy excitement.

Sasha turns around and when she sees us, she asks, "Can I help you?"

It's so strange to hear her voice this close, like she's an actual real person in real life. Which she is, obviously. But it's so crazy to see someone you see on TV all the time up so close. She doesn't seem like she could be the same person who went to my school and sat in the library and ate in the cafeteria and probably got chipped at least once. I mean, everyone gets chipped at least once—even me. Even Ross.

Dina and I are just standing there, silent for what feels like a million years. I expect Dina to talk first, but she's not, and I wonder if I should say something.

Finally, Dina opens her backpack and takes out the Rockwood Hills Middle School yearbook, the one from Sasha's sixth-grade year.

"So, you don't know us, Ms. Preston, but we actually know a lot about you," Dina says.

Sasha's eyes bulge, and I try to discreetly hit Dina. She sounds like a crazy stalker. What is she doing?

"Let me rephrase that." She clears her throat. "I'm Dina, and this is my friend Chelsea. We go to Rockwood Hills Middle School."

Dina just called me her friend again. Maybe we are friends. I'm having more fun with Dina today than I've had with my real friends in pretty much forever.

"Who allowed you to come find me here? Drake?" Sasha picks up her cell phone.

"No, wait, please," I say, suddenly feeling the confidence to actually say something. "Just listen to us. Do you have a minute to talk?"

At this moment, I am so proud of myself for speaking up. I feel like I have Dina to thank for that.

She backs up a few steps. "Just tell me how you got over here. Okay? I was your age once. I know what kids do. But please, I need to know if people are searching for you, if you ran away from home or something."

She was our age only a few years ago. Come on, Sasha.

Dina laughs. "No, it's nothing like that," she says.

"Are you sure?" Sasha asks.

"Yes, totally sure," I jump in to the conversation. "By the way, I love that Nanette Lepore dress you wore in the latest issue of *Us Weekly*."

"She's my favorite," Sasha says. Immediately, it seems like we have a bond, like fashion has brought us together.

"Mine, too." I need to think of something more interesting to say. "Is it super weird to be famous?"

It's kind of a dumb question, but I'm really curious.

"At times, yes." Sasha looks around. "Follow me," she says, leading us in the direction of all the trailers. "I need to get my tea. I can't drink the stuff they have out here, so I make my own. And I want to be awake for our conversation."

Dina nudges me with her elbow, like she's so happy because everything's working out.

It does feel good for things to work out every once in a while, but I'm not totally convinced we're there yet. Sasha could be lying to us, saying to follow her to her trailer so she can make her tea but really leading us to security or to the New York City Police Department.

We could be on our way to getting arrested for breaking and entering or stalking! Then my parents will have something else to be depressed and angry about. Kendall and Molly and their moms will be gossiping about it for years, and I'll be in worse shape than I was before.

19

DINA

Video tip: It's not necessary to put the person's name on-screen every time someone talks, just the first time.

Perfect—finally a time I can check my phone. Because as exciting as the movie set is, I'm still a bit panicked that I'm about to get grounded for life. And I've never been grounded before, not even once.

We're following Sasha, too excited or nervous to talk. I take my phone out of my pocket and see the little text message icon and the number 2 next to it. The first is a text from my mom.

Hope you are having fun. Love, Mom

I laugh out loud. She doesn't get the fact that you don't need to sign text messages. But—*phew.* At least she's not mad at me. Not yet anyway. Maybe she really doesn't suspect anything!

There's also a text from Ali.

> called ur house and ur dad said ur out with a friend
> fiona. who is fiona? u have a secret life on LI! call me
> l8r.

Ali's imagination gets the best of her almost all the time. Once last year she thought my dad was actually in the FBI because he was going on a business trip and I wasn't allowed to say where. He was actually surprising Ali's dad with a golfing weekend in Hilton Head, and that's why I couldn't say anything. Ali was freaked for weeks before and thought we were being investigated.

"I think we're in trouble," Chelsea says as soon as we're in Sasha's trailer. We're sitting in two directors chairs in the corner, and we're waiting for Sasha to get back with her tea. "I don't think she's getting tea. I think she's calling the police."

"But you just bonded about Nanette Lepore," I say, trying to get her to stay calm.

She shouldn't be thinking about the police. We're in Sasha's trailer. Really and truly in Sasha Preston's trailer, on a real movie set. I thought it would take me until I was at least twenty-five to get on a movie set, but here I am—at thirteen. Unbelievable. Un-bee-lee-va-ble.

Chelsea's biting her pinkie nail. "Well, yeah. But I don't

know. Maybe we overdid it. Maybe we're really stalkers. Stalking is illegal, you know."

I shake my head. "We didn't show up at her house wearing masks or anything. We were just on a public street. And we managed to find the craft services table, and she invited us in here."

"We snuck onto the set," she says, more forcefully now.

"Shhh," I tell her. "Just go with it."

"Okay." Chelsea smiles, and it's not the usual forced smile she gives me. It seems like a genuine smile, like she's actually having fun. I never really thought this would happen—the two of us having fun together. But I think it is.

Sasha gets back with her tea and pulls up a chair. I immediately feel better and think we're on the right track until we hear a knock on the door.

"Sasha, need you in five," the person says.

"Girls, I'm sorry. That's my cue." She sips her tea. "As much as I appreciate you coming to find me, I think I have to get back to work."

Chelsea and I look at each other. This is how it ends? This is how close we got only to get nowhere at all? And right when I realized that Chelsea and I were having fun.

She smiles. "Why don't you go out the back door? It'll be less chaotic."

We get up slowly and there's another knock on Sasha's door. This time she opens it. "Sasha, we need you now," a male voice says.

"Be right there, Drake. Thanks."

She keeps the door open a crack and turns around. I guess she's looking to make sure we're leaving. I guess this really isn't happening. I failed. I totally failed. We got so close, though—that's the worst part of it.

"Where are those two kids we sent to makeup?" We hear someone yell. "That was fifteen minutes ago. They're slowing down this whole scene! Drake, have you contacted makeup to find out about those two kids?" the voice says.

"No idea, Mickey. Hold on a minute."

"Tell the extras to take a break. We gotta find those kids. We're never using this casting agency again. This is ridiculous."

"Sash, take a few minutes," Drake says. "Some of the extras are missing." He shakes his head. "Insane."

Sasha closes the door and looks at us. Maybe it's that she notices the silly grins we have on our faces or maybe she's just quick to put two and two together.

"Extras?"

"You could say that," I tell her. "Can we please talk to you for a second?"

She sighs. "You know I'm in the middle of a workday, right? Actors and actresses are working when they're on a movie set."

We nod.

"Please," I say in my nicest voice. I wish Chelsea would say something, but she isn't speaking. I don't know if she's scared or bored or what. "We came in from Rockwood Hills. We're working on this video for the fiftieth anniversary. We really need—"

"Oh, you're the people who called my agent!" she says, yelling and almost laughing at the same time. "Girls, I'm so sorry, but I don't think I have the time to devote to that."

"No, it's not what you think," Chelsea says. It's not much, but at least she finally opened her mouth. She's been silent since we got into Sasha's trailer.

"Look, we're not asking you to be in it. We're not asking you to do anything for us. We just need to talk to you," I plead. "I know it seems weird. Two kids coming in here, trying to get you to talk, but think back to when you were in eighth grade. Think back to the kinds of stuff you went through."

There's a long pause. I don't know what else to say.

"We can talk," she says finally. "Just wait here for a few minutes, okay?" She gets up and walks outside. We hear her talking to Drake, but we can't exactly make out what she's saying.

"Can you believe this?" I ask Chelsea.

"I can't. Seriously. You're like some kind of mastermind."

I laugh.

"No, really. First of all, you figured out where this movie was shooting. Then you figured out how to get here and how to get onto the set. And now you're getting Sasha Preston to talk to us!" Chelsea raises her hand to high-five me. "I don't know anyone else like you."

"I'm just awesome."

"I guess so." She smiles like she means it. "You *are* pretty awesome."

And it's so, so good to hear. But I couldn't have done it without her coming along with me. And the truth is—the day has been really fun, like a constant adventure.

I want to say, *Then how come you don't invite me to hang out? How come I can't go to the movies with you and Kendall and Molly and Ross Grunner?* I want to say all these things. Because even though we're in Sasha Preston's trailer, I'm still the new girl in eighth grade. I'm still the girl who had to start school a month late. I'm still the girl with no friends.

It's funny how you can be doing something totally amazing

and yet the blahs of your life still creep into your brain and affect you.

Still, I'm feeling pretty proud of myself right now.

I don't know exactly how I did it, but I did it. We're in here. We're going to talk to Sasha Preston. She's going to talk to us. We're going to make an amazing video.

20

CHELSEA

Sasha Preston piece of advice: If you're at risk
of hurting someone's feelings, white lies
are okay. But be careful.

The people with the headsets keep saying they can't
finish the scene till they find those two kids, so we really
don't have a choice but to go and get our makeup done and
then do the scene. Our little trick of pretending to be extras
actually got us to be extras!

Sasha says she'll talk to us when the scene is over and
we all have a break. I've spent so many hours thinking about
what I'd ask Sasha if we ever got the chance to talk to her,
and now that it's here, I'm worried I'll forget everything I
wanted to ask.

Being extras wasn't at all what we thought would happen
today, but it's really cool. We're going to be in a real movie.

Dina and me, together as extras and sleuths and go-getters.

They do our makeup in a really simple way, just covering up blemishes and adding some color to our cheeks, and then they send us back to that strip of sidewalk where we just walk back and forth a million times.

Sometimes they tell us to smile, or pretend that we're talking to each other. They give us backpacks to sling over our shoulders and we're supposed to look like we're on our way home from school.

It's actually pretty funny.

Finally, we're done shooting the scene and all the extras are standing around.

A bulky guy comes over and says, "You guys signed your release forms?"

Dina nods.

The guy leaves.

"We did?" I ask Dina.

"No, but if we sign something now, they'll find out we weren't even supposed to be extras, so we really can't do that. It's not a big deal. It's just that we won't get paid."

Too bad—I could really use the money.

When the scene's over, we go back into Sasha's trailer. I look at the clock and notice that it's already after five.

"Do you know what time it is?" I ask Dina.

"No clue. But I should check my phone again. I felt it vibrating, but couldn't exactly answer it while we were shooting the scene."

Dina looks at her phone, and I look at mine.

Two texts from Ross.

> r u going to kendall's 2nite?

> why r u ignoring me?

A text from Molly.

> we need to talk to u tonite. come 2 kendall's. ordering in sushi. boys may come.

A text from my mom.

> We are going to Riverbay with the Cohens. ☺ can you please keep an eye on Alexa?

After I read that, I feel on top of the world. It's pathetic, but it's true. I am so happy my parents have plans. And I can tell my mom is happy also; she even put a smiley face in her text message! She is so high-tech! I don't even mind babysitting Alexa. First of all, I don't mind because I'm so happy my parents have plans, and I also don't mind because this means I can get out of going to Kendall's and dealing with whatever they have to talk to me about.

"Do you think I can go sneak outside? I have to call my mom back. She's called six times," Dina says, and for the first time since I met the girl, she actually looks nervous.

"Yeah, I guess you can," I say. "We're allowed to be in here right now. Aren't we?"

She nods and gets up but doesn't say anything else. Sasha is still in the back area of the trailer changing, and I feel a little silly just sitting here by myself. I'm tempted to walk around and look at her photos and makeup and other stuff, but that just seems wrong.

So I text Kendall and Ross the same thing:

> can't make it 2 nite. need to babysit alexa.

Kendall doesn't respond, but Ross does, in about three seconds.

> can I stop by? I'll walk over. I'll be at Drew's anyway.

Drew is Ross's best friend and one of the guys on the fringes of our little group. He lives next door to me, and we used to take baths together when we were little, which really grosses me out now when I think about it. He's the guy that everyone's just friends with and no one really ever wants to go out with him.

I write back:

I wonder what my parents would think about Ross coming over while they're out. It's never come up before, so I never asked. We always hang out in groups, and my house used to be the place where everyone hung out, so people were always over. But now it's always Kendall's house. I know it's because I really don't want people at my house, but still.

I wonder what it will be like to be alone with Ross. I wonder if he really likes me like everyone says. It's weird; yeah, he's cool and everything, but it's hard to see him as anything other than the boy who ate a crayon when we were six and the first boy who asked me to dance at the carnival in fifth grade.

I get excited thinking about it, though, and I'm happy to be excited about something. I'm happy to be happy about my parents having plans. I'm even happy about the fact that we were just extras and now we're just hanging out in Sasha Preston's trailer.

Dina comes back in and she looks all shaky. She keeps pushing her hair back and fiddling with one of her earrings.

"Are you okay?" I ask.

"Well, my parents seemed a little suspicious when they hadn't heard from me all day, and then my mom took my brother to his soccer game and she ran into all these moms from school there. She mentioned that I was with someone named Fiona, and they all said there's no Fiona in the grade. I should've picked a more common name." Dina sits down next to me. "So now they totally don't believe me, so I had to say something. So I said I was in the city with you and we were working on the project, but they still didn't believe me and they're really, really mad and they want me home right away."

"Wow. Are you okay?"

She shakes her head. "I mean, I'm already in huge trouble, so I feel like we should stay and talk to Sasha, right? If we go home now, we'll never be able to talk to her again." She moves closer to me and whispers, "Where is she anyway?"

"Still changing." I don't say anything about leaving—not when we're so close to our goal. But then I feel bad for Dina getting in trouble. I'm not sure what to do or say.

She slumps back in the chair and throws her hands up. "Let's just stay. I'm already grounded for the rest of my life. It doesn't matter."

A little part of me feels bad for her because she's done so much to get us here and now she's in trouble, and it's all because she doesn't really have any friends to say that she's with.

"Too bad you're grounded. I was going to invite you over tonight. I have to babysit my sister," I say without really thinking about it. Is that even true? I'm not sure. But it seems like just the thing to cheer her up. I don't like to see her upset.

"Really? That would have been awesome."

Finally, Sasha comes out and interrupts our conversation.

"Okay, girls, let's talk," she says, pulling up a chair to sit next to us. "First of all, tell me what grade you're in and what this project is about. Tell me everything."

Dina and I look at each other. "You go first," I say. I figure it's the least I can do.

"So, we've been assigned to make this video for the school's fiftieth anniversary: a day in the life of a Rockwood Hills student. And I figured a good way to start was to look at old yearbooks," Dina tells Sasha. "And that's when we found you."

"She means, that's when *she* found you," I interrupt. I think it's important for Sasha to know that, otherwise she'd think I was living under a rock my whole life. "I knew you went to our school."

Sasha laughs. "Oh, okay. So how can I help you for the video?"

I look at Dina and she looks at me, and neither of us says anything. She should be the one talking now, the one who worked so hard to find her and then get us here. I don't know why she's so quiet all of a sudden, but it seems like there are words on the tip of her tongue, she's just not saying them.

Finally, she opens her mouth again. "Well, what was your life like at Rockwood Hills? Did you love it? Hate it?"

After she asks that, it occurs to me that it's really not something I ever thought about before. School was just school and I liked it because all of my friends were around, but also because it was the only school I ever went to, the only place I knew.

I wonder if everyone spends time thinking about if they're happy somewhere, if things could be better somewhere else. Of course, I realize it's not the best place in the world right now, but I guess it used to be, before all the bad stuff happened.

I remember all the stuff I wanted to ask Sasha—about her friends, her social life, what it was like to go to Rockwood Hills when she did.

"I'll wait until you're ready," Sasha says.

I look at Dina. What is she talking about? We're ready, duh. We just asked her the question.

When we don't respond to that, Sasha asks, "So are you recording this?" She looks at Dina and then at me. "Isn't that the point? I'm going to be in the video?" She laughs again. "Sorry if I'm confused; it's just kids don't usually come find me for help on a school project."

"Oh, yeah, well, we could put it in the video," I say. "That could be the opening!"

Dina takes out the camera and pushes Record. To be

honest, I'm not sure it's the right thing for the video, or the way to start it, or anything since I basically know nothing about video. But not recording it would be stupid. It's a once-in-a-lifetime chance.

Sasha takes a deep breath and then starts talking. "When I started sixth grade at Rockwood Hills Middle School, I was like any other girl. I had friends. I loved school. All was fine. I was really into singing, and I took piano lessons and it was all good."

Dina and I are just sitting here silently, nodding. We don't want to interrupt her—well, I don't want to interrupt her, that's all I know.

"But around seventh grade, things began to change. It was kind of a weird time of people drifting away from things that always seemed normal and steady," she says, like she's answering my question without me even having to ask it. "Everyone just kind of wanted to be the same as everyone else. I was suddenly this weird girl for wanting to play piano in the talent show."

So that explains it, how she seemed to have BFFs her first two years and then was a loner her last year.

"That was something I really wanted to ask you," I jump in. "Like, how do you get things to stay the same?"

"They can't. Things are always changing and evolving," she tells us.

"I mean, like, one day everything's perfect and the next

day it's not." I bite my bottom lip. "So what do you do in that situation?"

She looks at me with crinkly eyes, like she's confused and doesn't know what to answer, and then we get interrupted. "Sasha, we need you for a scene in ten," a guy says after knocking on her door.

"Okay," she yells back. Then to us she says, "I'll speed up my story. I hope this will help answer some of the questions you have, and help with the video in some way."

"Oh, it is," Dina tells her. "And I play piano, too."

I smile because that's a nice little fact that Dina decided to share, but now that I've gotten the courage to ask Sasha my questions, I really want her to answer them.

"So, over time, my friends and I kind of drifted apart. But then I started auditioning and moved to the city, and, well, that was the end of my time at Rockwood Hills." She shrugs. "I just didn't really fit in; I couldn't find my niche. Maybe if you were there when I was in eighth grade, I wouldn't have hated it so much. Maybe we could have been friends."

That's a pretty awesome thing to hear. Sasha Preston would have been friends with us! How amazing is that?

"Are you guys best friends?" she asks.

"Uh," Dina stammers.

I didn't see this coming. I answer without really thinking

about what I was going to say, "We were just assigned to work on this project together."

I hope that didn't sound so totally mean, but it's the truth, and that's why I said it.

"So, to answer your question," Sasha says, looking at me. "Things really can't stay the same forever. And you just have to do your best to keep up with the changes."

"How do you think we could make the video good?" Dina asks, and it's kind of obvious she wants to change the topic and get it back to the video. "On your show you're always giving advice. And I know that's a character, but maybe you have advice?"

"You should probably try to focus on a wide range of kids in the school. Oh, and once you tell them it's for a project, people won't be honest and it won't seem real. Just be casual, get the stories when you can," Sasha says. "Pay attention to what goes on around you."

The thing about Rockwood Hills is that the different groups of kids don't talk to each other. I wonder if it was like that when Sasha went there. I know the other kids and have known them my whole life, but we just don't talk.

If I saw them outside of school in the mall or something, maybe I'd say hi. But seeing them in school, passing in the hallway, never. We'd never, ever say hi.

It's just the way it is.

"Well, I've tried," Dina says, sounding defensive. "The only thing is, I don't really know anyone because I'm new this year. And people get quiet when they see the video camera."

"I see." Sasha sighs and readjusts herself in her chair. "Being new someplace is never easy . . . Oh, I just remembered something! Do they still 'chip' people?" She makes quotation mark signs with her fingers when she says it. "That was so cruel. I definitely don't miss that."

"Yeah, I've been chipped five times already. And I've only been there a month and a half," Dina admits. "Rockwood Hills is nothing like my old school. I was cool there. Here, I don't have any friends, really. Oh, and I lied to my parents about where I was today to be able to come here."

I don't know why I can't say anything else. I feel like it's obvious that I'm just sitting here not adding anything more to the conversation, but I kind of feel like a third wheel all of a sudden. Dina's in charge of the video, and Sasha's the celebrity . . . and I'm just, like, here.

"Hmm. It sounds tough," Sasha says, looking at her watch. "What about you?" She turns to me. "Do you like the school?"

I guess I have to speak now. "Well, that's the thing I was talking about before." I stop myself for a second and think about what to say next. "I mean, it's okay," I say. "I've lived in the neighborhood since kindergarten, so I know a lot of people."

"You really just think it's *okay?*" Dina blurts out, not letting me really finish what I was going to say, seeming like she's mad or trying to start a fight with me. "You have a million friends. Everyone thinks you have the perfect life. Even Ross likes you. Why is it just *okay?*"

"What are you saying?" my face tightens, and I feel like I could start crying any moment. "Why are you getting so worked up?"

Dina doesn't answer me; she turns to Sasha instead. "She's popular, so she likes it, but I don't know why she won't admit that. The truth is, if you're popular, school is great. If you're not, it's awful. That's it."

I try to take a deep breath and try to say something to defend myself, but I can't.

Dina turns to Sasha and says, "Even on your show, it's a high school, but it's the same thing. You obviously love the school because you give advice and everyone knows you. But that character Martha—come on, she's such a loser. Everyone makes fun of her."

Sasha laughs. "Okay. First of all, that's television."

"It resembles real life, doesn't it?" Dina asks.

"But the thing is, you guys have the power to change things," Sasha says. "That's what I didn't realize then and only realize now because I'm a little older. No one speaks up and that's why nothing changes. Everyone just goes along with it and no one says anything. But I bet more people feel like you than you realize."

She's only a few years older than us, and she talks like a mom. I guess her celebrity status has gone to her head.

Sasha must've read my mind because she says, "Really, you *can* make it better. Trust me." She takes a deep breath. "I'm so glad you guys came and found me." She winks. "Now go home and try to get out of your punishment," she tells Dina. "Your parents will forgive you sooner or later."

"You think?" Dina asks.

"I know."

21

DINA

Video tip: Keep words on the screen long
enough for people to read them twice.

"This has been an amazing day," Chelsea says once
we're on the train. "I know this sounds cheesy, but thank you."

I laugh. "It doesn't sound cheesy. It's good to hear."

We sit back in our seats and stare out the window as we
wait for the conductor to come and punch our tickets.

"It *has* been a totally amazing day," I say after a few seconds
of silence.

Chelsea sighs. "It felt good to talk to Sasha, didn't it?"

I nod. "Totally."

"Because she's a real person who went to our school and
things weren't always great for her, but she graduated and look
how she's doing now." Chelsea seems so serious all of a sudden.
"Even if things are bad, they can get better. Ya know?"

I nod. I'm not sure if Chelsea thinks I know what she's referring to. I feel like this is one of those instances where I should just sit and listen.

It's hard to tell if Chelsea realizes how people see her, how when you're popular your life is made—or at least that's how it seems.

As we get closer and closer to Rockwood Hills, I stop thinking about this because I am getting more and more nervous.

I was never the type of girl to do bad things, so I was never the type of girl to get in trouble.

I have no idea what's in store for me.

My parents are there waiting when we get off the train, and Chelsea's mom is waiting, too. Chelsea and I say good-bye quickly. I tell her to have fun with Ross. I try not to be too jealous that she has actual plans on a Saturday night—and plans with Ross, of all people.

Ali and I would always talk about what life would be like on Long Island and one of the things that always came up was that I'd have boys over. Ali said I'd be babysitting Nathan and a boy would walk over and we'd make microwave popcorn and watch a movie on one of the leather couches in my den.

Too bad that hasn't happened yet. Too bad it's never going to happen.

For one thing, I haven't even babysat since we've been here. My grandparents always come over to stay with us.

For another, I have no friends to come over—let alone boyfriends.

I reach for the car door handle, and I feel like I'm going in slow motion. I get into the car, sit down, and buckle my seat belt, and my dad starts to drive home.

"Hi," I say. "First of all, I'm really sorry for lying. You have every right to be really, really, really mad at me." I think it's best to start out apologizing; then it doesn't really leave them with that much to say.

"We appreciate your apology," my mom says. "And we're glad you know lying is wrong."

Then: nothing. They don't say anything. I stare at the clock above the radio. The minutes tick by. My dad is silent. So is my mom. What is going on?

"So what's my punishment?" I ask. I have to know. Waiting and not knowing is probably way harder than just being punished.

"Just don't do it again," my dad says.

"What?" I ask.

"Don't do it again," he repeats.

I can't believe this. They sounded furious on the phone. I was nervous all day. And there's no punishment? That's so not like them. They really believe in the punishment-fitting-the-crime kind of discipline. I don't know what's gotten into them.

"We know you're having a rough time, honey," my mom says. "We're just glad you made plans with someone. But we wish you could have just been honest about it."

"Really? No punishment?" I should be happy about this, but instead I'm just confused.

"We'll discuss more when we get inside," my dad says, pulling into the driveway.

My grandparents are at our house, and for the first time in my life, I feel embarrassed to see them. I feel like they won't look at me the same way anymore. They'll see me as some rebellious teenager instead of the nice girl they used to know.

It's strange—now that my parents aren't that mad at me, I'm even madder at myself.

My grandparents are taking Nathan out to dinner, so luckily they don't have a lot of time to look at me as the rebellious teenager. My parents and I sit down in the den, and we start talking.

It feels like one of those "talks" you see on TV, like on Sasha's show. Sasha's always getting in trouble with her parents—that's what most of her advice is about.

"We're not going to punish you because we don't think you did it to be purposefully deceitful, but we'd like to understand why you did it," my dad says.

"I didn't think you'd let me go to the city, and I couldn't risk that. I had to go for my project," I tell them. "And so I figured it was best to just go and come back."

My mom moves closer to me on the couch and puts her arm around me. "Please just be honest with us from now on. Actually, starting now! How are you doing? How are things at school? You seem so distant and so unlike you."

I want to open up to them and tell them how hard it is to find friends and how Chelsea doesn't even consider me a real friend. But somehow I just can't. Maybe it's because I'm tired. Maybe it's because I need to process the day or because all I can think about is Chelsea and Ross Grunner. Even with the stuff about her dad, her life is so much better than mine.

"I promise to be honest from now on," I tell them. "But I'm really tired now. Can I go upstairs and lie down?"

"Sure," my mom says. "We're going to dinner with that couple from down the street, the Bentens. You'll be okay here? Do you want to invite a friend over or something?"

"Maybe," I say as I'm walking up the stairs. "I'll think about it."

And even with that talk about honesty, I just lied again. Because I won't think about it, not because I don't want to, but because I don't have anyone to invite.

22

CHELSEA

Sasha Preston piece of advice: Don't burn
bridges. You never know when you'll
change your mind about someone.

My parents look so happy going out that I almost forget
what's really going on: that my dad spent the whole day (up
until an hour ago) in his workout clothes, that my mom
cashed in an IRA to pay for the rest of Alexa's braces. I don't
think I'm really supposed to know this, but I overheard them
refer to it while they were getting ready.

My dad's wearing one of his pinstriped sports jackets and
a peach tie, and my mom has on her black pants with her
sequined sweater. I want to take a picture of them so I can
remember how they look, just in case they never look this way
again. I'm not even a sentimental person, but this whole thing
with my dad has started to turn me into one.

"Call us if there's a problem," my mom says. "And there's money for pizza on the kitchen counter. Alexa should be busy with that dollhouse video game Grandma sent her, but it wouldn't hurt if you paid a little attention to her."

"Got it."

"Are you having Kendall and the girls over?" my dad asks.

"Not sure yet." I shrug. Now I'm turning into Dina and becoming a liar. It's not even hard—it just seems to happen all of a sudden. "We'll see. I may catch up on homework, and I also have that project for the fiftieth anniversary to work on."

"Good girl," he says.

And then a blissful few seconds later, they're out the door on the way to Riverbay, where they spent so many Saturday nights in the good old days.

Maybe this is a sign that things are changing, that things will return to normal soon, and that everything will be okay again. And maybe Ross and I will start going out tonight, like we're supposed to, and that will be a good distraction, too. I could always start to like him more once we're going out. It seems like meeting Sasha Preston was my good luck charm. Ever since this morning, things have been getting better.

Ross rings the bell at eight forty-seven, and it's clear that he didn't want to arrive exactly at eight forty-five but didn't want to be late, either. That's so Ross.

My skin starts to feel prickly thinking about the fact that I have a guy over and my parents don't know, even though it's just Ross and they've known Ross forever. It's just that when I usually have guys over, there are girls over, too.

But I'm in eighth grade now! This is what eighth graders are supposed to do.

"Hey," he says, walking into my house like he lives here. "What's up? How was *el ciudad?*"

"Practicing your Spanish?" I laugh.

"Sí." He smiles. "So how was it? And can I have one of those graham cracker granola bars you're always eating in math? They look soooooo good."

"Sure." He follows me into the kitchen, and I start telling him all about the day, how much of a sleuth Dina is and how we actually ended up being extras in the movie, which I still can't believe.

He seems really interested. Interested like a girl would be, not like an eighth-grade boy. It's weird to see him alone, without anyone else around. He seems calmer and less worried about impressing people. "So, how did Dina find out all this stuff? And were you totally nervous about sneaking into the extras scene and into the trailer and all of that?" He climbs up onto one of our kitchen barstools and finishes his graham cracker granola bar in one bite.

"I have no clue how she figured it out." I shrug and don't answer about how nervous I was. Ross doesn't need to know that. "She's a detective."

"Really?"

"No. I mean, she's not like a paid detective." I laugh. "But she can find out anything, probably about people at school, too. Like if Mr. Oliver was really involved in that scandal with the rigged tennis team tryouts."

Ross throws his head back and bangs his hand on the counter. "That was ridiculous!" He widens his eyes like he's in some kind of spooky horror film. "You think she's found out stuff about me?"

Ross seems really interested in what Dina thinks of him. I think he must be fascinated with new people. We've all been in the same classes with the same kids since kindergarten, for the most part, so we're used to each other. "I doubt it."

"Why?" He has a stupid grin on his face, and it makes me want to throw something at him. Maybe I can't go out with Ross Grunner. Maybe he's just as annoying as everybody else.

"I don't know." I look at this colorful painting on the wall. My mom bought it in Spain when my parents were there a few years ago. After I stare at it for a few seconds, it starts to give me a headache. "Anyway, why'd you come over here? What do you want to talk to me about?"

I walk around the island in my kitchen and sit down on the barstool next to his. Up close he smells like he used too much cologne or too much of that men's body spray.

"I just wanted to see how you're doing," he says. "I mean, it totally sucks that you're, like, faced with this whole new lifestyle now."

I raise my eyebrows at him, but he keeps talking. "You know, all the stuff you were used to, you can't really get anymore, and everyone knows about it, and it's just sucky. It's like your parents were involved in some kind of scandal."

"Not really," I say. "They didn't do anything wrong. If you watched the news, you'd see it's a pretty bad economy out there."

"You watch the news?" Ross scoffs. "Chelsea Stern watches the news?"

I shrink away from him a little. "Sometimes," I mumble.

"That's hard to picture." He laughs. "So, how are you handling it?"

"Well, I'm not exactly homeless," I tell him, annoyed that he just laughed at me. "I mean, yeah, I'm dealing with fewer pairs of jeans, but I'm not going to school in rags."

This is what I don't get about Rockwood Hills. In any other part of the country, everyone would know that people are losing their jobs, and it wouldn't be the biggest deal and no one would treat it like you had some kind of highly contagious disease.

I know Ross came over here to help me, supposedly, but he doesn't seem to understand any more than Kendall and Molly do.

"Chelsea." He lowers his eyes at me, and I suddenly think this is a really bizarre time for a first kiss with someone. "Come on. You know and I know that we were the richest kids in the grade."

Barf. I want to barf right now. I hate this discussion. How was I ever a person who was okay with talking about that stuff? And when did I change?

I don't respond. Ross takes another granola bar out of the box, and I wonder if we should order in pizza. I look at the clock and see it's after nine o'clock. He must be starving. Alexa must be starving, too.

"Alexa!" I shout down to the basement. "What do you want on your pizza?"

I hear the twinkling sounds of her new dollhouse video game. You get points every time you finish decorating a room. She probably would have forgotten about dinner altogether if I hadn't reminded her.

"Mushrooms!" she yells back, and Ross mouths the word *mushrooms* like it's weird.

"What kind of kid eats mushrooms?" he asks.

"Oh, now mushrooms are for poor people?" I say, mostly

kidding but a little curious about how he'll respond to that.

"I never said you were poor," he says all matter-of-factly. "I'm sure your dad's severance package was more than most people make in a whole year, maybe even two years."

How does he know all of this? "Do you read the *Wall Street Journal* or something?"

"I do, actually," he says, all smug and proud of himself.

Right now he looks so cute, and I start to think I can actually like him like that. It's bizarre how these feelings can change in a second, like turning a car engine on and off.

I can't think of anything else to say, and I guess he can't, either. "Where's your computer?" he asks, out of nowhere.

"Upstairs on my desk. Why?"

"I wanna show you something. I'll be right back," he says.

"Great. I'll order the pizza."

As soon as he's gone and out of the kitchen, I start to get a creepy feeling that he's upstairs in my room all by himself. Is he looking through my stuff? Touching my pillows? He's still a boy, after all, and who knows what gross things boys do.

I try not to think about it. Instead, I order two pizzas and two bottles of soda, and the guy on the phone tells me it'll be here in thirty minutes.

While Ross is upstairs getting my computer, I start to wonder if I've really changed, if this whole thing with my dad's job has turned me into a different person. Because I don't think I can be the same person anymore, someone who only cares about having fancy, expensive stuff and going on exotic vacations every single school break. Maybe that's what makes people change. Things in their life change, and so they have to become different.

Maybe that's really obvious to most people, but it just occurred to me.

Take Dina, for example. Maybe she's become this new person who lies to her parents because she had to move, and she'll never be the same as the girl she used to be back wherever she used to live. Maybe at the end of the year, she'll be different from how she is now. Maybe we're always just changing, and we don't even realize it until after the change has happened.

"Ready?" Ross asks, poking his head into the kitchen.

"For?"

"To watch videos on the *Wall Street Journal* site. Duh. It's not what you think—all boring, financial stuff. There are cool videos on the site, too. Come sit on the couch." He walks into the den and makes himself comfortable, like he's the one who lives here and I'm the guest.

"Sure, but the pizza will be here in thirty minutes," I tell him.

He nods and starts the video. We're sitting so close to each other on the couch. Now I'm definitely sure he used too much cologne, and I can't figure out if I love him or hate him or even like him. I can't figure out who I am and if I've changed, and I have no idea why we're watching *Wall Street Journal* videos on a Saturday night.

None of this makes sense. All my friends are at Kendall's, eating sushi and having a sleepover and pranking people in the grade, and I'm alone with Ross Grunner on my couch. But I don't want to be either place.

What do I want?

"Why are we watching this?" I ask.

"You didn't believe me that I actually read it." Ross laughs and moves a little closer to me on the couch. His breath smells like graham crackers from the granola bars. "But don't worry, my family makes fun of me all the time for it, too. They think I'm totally right-wing, but they're just super liberal."

"Your family is super liberal?" I ask. I'm not even really sure I know what liberal means, but I don't think it's how I'd describe the Grunners.

"Here, let's watch this clip about a billion-dollar resort in China," he says.

So I sit back and watch and try as hard as I can not to think about anything else.

Lately, I'm always waiting for something to happen. Right now I'm definitely waiting for something to happen, but I'm not even sure I know what I'm waiting for.

23

DINA

Video tip: Start with an establishing shot—
a general shot of the subject or location
to help define the project.

At lunch on Monday, the Acceptables are talking about what they always talk about—Chelsea Stern and Ross Grunner.

"She's so different this year, though," Maura says. Maura has tuna salad in her braces, and if I look at it too closely, it makes me queasy. "She doesn't even seem to care about the trends, or what everybody's wearing, or anything."

"I don't think she's that different," Katherine says. "Her jeans cost more than my whole back-to-school wardrobe."

Katherine lives in the Spruce section. I think they may rent out the basement of their house to someone else. Her dad owns a lumberyard, and her mom's a nurse. She's always talking about the money situation in Rockwood Hills and how some people have so much more than others. But Katherine's the one with the sandwiches from the deli every day for lunch, all wrapped up in their perfect white paper. Her mom gets them for her on the way to school. It's a small thing for a mom to do, but I think it's really nice.

I've been sitting with these girls for over a month now, and all they talk about is grades and Chelsea Stern. They're so predictable that sometimes I make up stories about the secret lives they could lead. Like Katherine runs to the city on the weekends to play competitive poker, and Maura secretly plays the electric guitar. Stuff like that.

"Dina, are you coming to my house on Saturday?" Maura asks. "We're going to order in Chinese and study for the science final."

"Dina's not in honors," Katherine says almost in a whisper, like it's some kind of horrible secret I've been trying to hide.

"Oh, right," Maura says. "No big deal. You can still study for yours. Just bring your books and notes and everything."

Thanks, Maura, I think to myself. *Thanks for telling me what I need to bring for a study session.*

I should be excited about this—the plans, I mean. It's the first time they've actually invited me over. But I don't get why we have to study on a Saturday night. The final isn't for weeks yet.

"Is that okay, Dina? Sorry," Maura says.

She's one of those girls who say sorry for everything. I don't think she's really sorry I'm not good at science.

"Yeah, it's fine," I say. "Didn't you say your brother has that new game system?"

She nods.

"Well, I can always just play that."

"Um." Maura laughs nervously. "Sure, whatever."

Across the cafeteria, Chelsea and her friends are talking and laughing, and one of their guy friends keeps getting up to bring the girls' table notes from the boys' table and vice versa.

Chelsea and I had so much fun chasing Sasha. Could these girls be that fun, too?

"Have you hung out with Chelsea outside of school?" Trisha asks, as if reading my mind. "Does she talk about Ross all the time?"

I don't want to tell them about Sasha Preston and our day in the city. They won't get it or think it's cool. They think Chelsea is more of a celebrity than Sasha is anyway.

I'm trying to think of how to answer that question when I feel someone come up behind me and put hands on my shoulders.

The whole table looks freaked out, which makes me freaked out. Almost too scared to turn around. But finally I do.

It's Ross.

"I heard you're a detective," he says.

All I can think about is that Ross is at our table. Maura, Trisha, and Katherine are just sitting there, staring at the two of us.

I'm worried they may pass out.

"Um," I say finally. "Well, I'm not like Sherlock Holmes." I laugh. I can't believe I just said that. How did I just come up with the stupidest response ever?

"I heard you're pretty good," Ross says.

Now what do I say? I don't know. Talking to Ross would be hard anyway, but it's even harder with the Acceptables sitting here, just staring at us.

Luckily, Mrs. O'Hanlon, the lunch aide, tells us that it's time to clean up, so I just say, "Well, gotta throw out the trash."

That's an even stupider response. What in the world is wrong with me?

As I'm throwing away my turkey sandwich remnants, I'm going over those four sentences—the entire conversation— again and again.

What will I tell the Acceptables now?

What if he comes over to the table again?

What does this all mean?

• • •

"I've been telling everybody about our day on Saturday," Chelsea says as soon as she sees me in the library after school.

"Really?" I ask, even though I figured that out after the Ross lunch interaction.

"Yes!" She drops her backpack on the table. "Kendall, c'mere."

Kendall's here? Kendall and I have never had a conversation. She's scarier than my math teacher.

"Yo yo yo yippee yo!" She runs over to us. Her Prada backpack is half open, and it looks like her books are about to fall all over the floor.

"You should work for Page Six or something," she tells me, not even saying hi first, and making it sound like an insult, even though it should really be a compliment. Page Six is this big gossip column that runs in one of the New York papers; my grandma's always talking about who was written up on Page Six.

I laugh. "Yeah, right."

"No, seriously." She pops her gum. "You're like a professional stalker. Chelsea's totally impressed. So is Ross."

Chelsea hits Kendall's arm after she says that. I feel like that arm hit was supposed to mean something, but I'm not sure what.

Kendall's charm bracelet makes clacking sounds against

the wooden library table, and I immediately want a charm bracelet just like it. Kendall and all her material possessions have that power over people. At least over me.

"I made a reservation at Gatsby's for your b-day, Chels," Kendall says while getting out her phone to text at the same time.

Gatsby's is this really cool restaurant in the downtown area of Rockwood Hills. It's named after the book *The Great Gatsby* because the book was set only ten minutes from here. So far that's the coolest thing about Rockwood Hills, and it's not even that cool because it didn't take place in this town; it took place ten minutes away.

Gatsby's has steak and lobster and all these exotic pasta dishes. They have live music on the weekends, too; Billy Joel played there when he was first getting his start, and also John Mayer. More recently, obviously. It's really hard to get reservations there. You have to book at least three months in advance. My dad wants to take my grandparents there for their anniversary, but he hasn't had any luck yet. I guess Kendall has connections.

"Anyway," Kendall continues, "I think we should invite the boys. It'll be easier."

I just sit here quietly making a list of possible angles for the fiftieth-anniversary project. One thought I had was to have only footage, no voice-over, just Sasha talking at the beginning and then shots of all the different kids. It could be powerful that way. I also had an idea that we'd have people say just one word that comes to mind when they think of Rockwood Hills Middle School and then we'd cut that together.

I have all these ideas, but I need to get Chelsea to agree to them.

They're still debating about whether they should invite the boys to the party, if it'll be easier or harder that way. I have no idea how inviting the boys makes anything easier. Or why it's even hard to have a birthday dinner in the first place.

All the birthday dinners I've ever had have been with my family and Ali. And they're not stressful at all.

"Fine, but if there's drama between Molly and Marcus, I'll be so annoyed," Chelsea says.

Do they even know I'm here? I mean, of course they know. But do they wonder what I'm doing? Why are they having this conversation in front of me?

"There won't be. It's your birthday, and I'm in charge." Kendall's phone bings three times, and she rolls her eyes at it.

"And I can't believe you already organized this. My b-day's not for two weeks. And at Gatsby's, Ken! That's amazing." Chelsea reaches out to hug her.

"Of course, love." Kendall smiles in the most over-the-top way, and when the hug separates, she air-smooches Chelsea.

Now Kendall's phone is ringing instead of binging. Who in the world needs to reach her so badly? She kisses Chelsea on the cheek (for real this time) and leaves the library. She doesn't say good-bye to me.

"Such drama," Chelsea says once Kendall's gone. I nod like I know what she means even though I have no idea whatsoever.

"Anyway, so we only have a few more weeks and I feel like I am even more clueless about this video now," she says, rolling her eyes. "Now that we found Sasha, which was great and all, it's, like, who even wants to do this anymore?"

"Um, I do." I force a smile.

"Oh." She pounds out a text message and looks back at me. "Do you have any ideas on how we can get this done?"

I do have ideas, but at the moment, I can't even process them or say them. All I'm thinking about is that her birthday is soon. I didn't even know that. And I'm not invited to her party. At least, I don't think I am.

All I get to do is hang out with the Acceptables and study for science.

I thought we were friends, but I guess we're not.

"Do you want to take over the project? It's okay with me, really," Chelsea says. "After all, this project is sort of your baby."

"It's your baby, too. Your assigned baby."

"Yeah. I actually gotta run," she says, like she didn't even hear what I just said. "So let's finalize a plan at lunch tomorrow. Eat fast, okay? I'll come by your table."

I nod. Part of me is excited; Chelsea Stern coming to my lunch table.

But the Acceptables were absolutely speechless when Ross came by our table. I can only imagine what Katherine, Maura, and Trisha are gonna say about this.

As soon as I feel like I can handle things here, everything gets shaken up again. Chelsea gets mean and Ross shows up out of nowhere and the Acceptables sometimes don't even seem that acceptable.

At my old school we'd do these science experiments where we'd put all these different liquids—seltzer, food coloring, and other stuff that I can't remember—into a big two-liter soda bottle, and then we'd shake it up to see what would happen when all the liquids mixed together.

That's what it feels like here, only I don't want to be doing the mixing. I want things to just settle—but settle in a good way—and then stay like that.

24

CHELSEA

Sasha Preston piece of advice: Use people's
names when you greet them.

"So I'm just going to put this out there," Ross says to
me on the phone. Lately, we've been talking most nights, and I
wanted to find out what he thought about having all the boys
at my birthday dinner, so I called him. Plus my parents are
at curriculum night for Alexa, so I can be sure there won't be
any fighting. I love nights like this. They're kind of rare now,
though they didn't used to be. "Tell me what you think about
Dina. Like, as a girl."

"As a girl?" I ask. "I don't get it."

"Come on, Chelsers, you know what I mean."

"I really don't."

"Would it be weird if I went out with her? 'Cuz, she's new,
and, you know, not in our group or anything."

"Are you serious?" I burst out laughing even though it's not funny and I'm not the kind of girl who bursts out laughing at stuff like this. I don't know why he's saying this to me, especially since Kendall and Molly and I have always talked about me and Ross going out. I can't figure out what I'm supposed to say, and this conversation is making me feel like I don't know anything, like if someone asked me what two plus two equaled, I wouldn't even know.

"She's never had a boyfriend," I say before my brain knows that I'm talking. "And she's only had made-up crushes. And she wears ugly jeans and these weird oversized T-shirts. And her hair isn't even in a real style; it's just long and curly and she usually wears it in a ponytail."

All he says is "Okay."

"And she's kind of a stalker," I continue. I can't stop now. "It's cool sometimes. But it's also weird."

"You didn't think it was weird before," he says. "But you're saying I shouldn't go out with her?"

"I can't even believe we're having this conversation," I mumble.

There's silence on the phone for a few moments.

"I could talk to her for you," I say, and I'm shocked that the words come out of my mouth, but once I start on this path, I can't stop. I'm not sure why I just offered that, exactly, but after I say it, I'm excited, like I'm still a part of what's going to happen.

I hate the way I sound now, all shaky and uncertain and insecure. Sometimes I've worried that Ross and I would have this conversation—but about Kendall or Molly, never about Dina.

"Okay, but don't be all awkward," he says. "We don't need to be all fourth-grade about it."

"I wouldn't be." I want to get off the phone with him. Right now. "I gotta go, Ross."

"Um. You okay, Chelsea?" he asks. "About Dina and all? I just figured that since you spend all this time with the girl working on that crazy video you'd be the best one to talk to about this, and I really don't know any of her friends."

"She doesn't have any friends," I say, and as soon as I say it I feel like the meanest person ever. I don't want to be this person, but it seems like she's taking over, like this personality owns me now.

"Harsh," he says. "Okay, later, Chelsers."

I used to like when he called me that. And now I hate it. Now I hate everything.

I thought things were better on Saturday, when I got to meet Sasha Preston and when my parents had plans and Ross was coming over, and then today Kendall's planning my birthday and getting a reservation at Gatsby's—it seemed like everything was normal and fun again.

But it's not.

In truth, things weren't better even though my parents did go out to eat, because when they got home, they were fighting about how my mom was so nervous the credit card would be declined. And then my dad kept saying that it wasn't declined, it was fine, and then my mom kept saying the worrying was just as bad, as if it had actually happened.

And then they fought for forty-seven minutes. I timed it.

And I know my parents will never be able to pay for everyone to go to Gatsby's for my birthday. I couldn't tell Kendall, because it was so nice and normal of her to make the reservation, but I was fooling myself.

Things aren't better.

Now Dina and I still have to work on this stupid project, and I have no idea what I'm going to do with her and Ross Grunner. They'll end up going out, I bet, and she'll end up being in my group, and everyone will like her better than they like me because she doesn't act nervous and worried all the time. She's actually pretty funny, and she does crazy things like they're not even a big deal, and even Kendall seems impressed with her now.

My parents get home from curriculum night a few minutes

later and I can tell things didn't go well because they come in silently except for the slamming of the front door.

"You were in a trance when the Malheims were talking to us," my mom says. "Did you see how they were looking at us?"

Silence from my dad.

"Bruce, please. You have to realize how you act," my mom goes on.

"I'm sorry, Dayna. I can't live up to your expectations of how you want people to see me, to see us," he says. "There's more to life than how others see you."

"That's not what I'm saying."

"You are. You want me to be an accessory of yours. Or I don't know what."

"I don't. I just hate when people look at us the way they're looking at us," my mom says.

"Which is what?"

"That pity look," she says.

"That's not my fault. It's theirs," my dad says, and I hear him walking up the stairs, away from my mom.

It's hard to tell who's right and who's wrong here or exactly what happened, and in the end I'm not really sure I want to know.

I get into bed and pretend to go to sleep, so that when

my mom comes in to say good night, I'll already be asleep and I won't have to talk to her.

Sure enough, she does knock on my door. When she peeks her head in, the lights are out and I'm pretending to be asleep.

Lately, I do a lot of pretending, and I'm not sure why or where it's getting me.

Hours and hours of me worrying and stressing and tossing and turning go by, and then I hear my phone vibrate with a text from Kendall.

> Have you checked out RHMS Facebook page?

Some kid who graduated last year started this unofficial, students-only page, and it has stupid posts about dances and fund-raisers, though it got more popular since people have been writing gossipy stuff on it. People like to read about other people's misfortunes. It's like the whole chipped thing— people like to see other people suffer.

At least the news about my dad wasn't posted on it. Not yet.

Kendall texts me again.

> Go look at it.

So I get out of bed, which isn't really a big deal since I wasn't even sleeping anyway, and when I sign into Facebook and look at the page, I know right away what she's done.

She posted the video of Dina, the one of her falling in the doorway of Mr. Valakis's classroom, with the train of toilet paper around her ankle.

And people have seen it. There are forty-two comments, and it's only been posted for ten minutes.

I text back:

> Why'd u do that?

Five minutes later, she writes back:

> she's weird. And it's funny.

I don't know why I do it—I'm not even sure I believe it—but I text her right back:

> HAHAHAHAHA. Good one, Ken.

I'm a terrible, awful person, and I would never admit this to anyone, but after what Ross said to me on the phone, I need Kendall to be my friend.

25

Dina

Video tip: When conducting an interview,
avoid yes-or-no questions.

I walk into school the next morning and I swear people are
staring at me. But they're not just staring—they're laughing,
too.

Then I turn my back for one second at my locker and
I'm chipped. Again. Totally caught off guard.

And then I'm walking to class and people are looking at
me, and I'm not just being self-conscious.

"Sorry that happened to you," Lee says in homeroom
as I'm shaking the potato chip crumbs out of my backpack
into the trash. I used to sneak into the bathroom stall to get
rid of the crumbs, but now I don't even bother.

"Oh, I'm used to it."

"You're used to people posting embarrassing videos of

you on Facebook and then the whole school watching and commenting?" She snickers. "Whoa, rough life! Rougher than I thought."

I step back a little and look around the room to see if there are any clues. I have no idea what she's talking about.

I go back to my seat and Lee has her laptop open and turned to me so I can see it. "You've seen this, right?" she asks me.

I look over at the screen. And I see myself. Falling. The toilet paper. All over again.

And the comments.

Weirdo

HAHAHAHA

What's wrong with her?

OMG. LOSER.

FUNNIEST THING EVER

That was the funniest thing that person has ever seen? Wow. There are so many things funnier than falling in a classroom doorway—like the time this girl, Phoebe Bonden, accidentally called me when her cell phone was in her pocket and I heard five minutes of this conversation she was having with her dad about toothpaste brands, or the time when my cousin was looking at the Pizzeria Uno menu upside down for like five minutes without realizing it, or the time Ali said, "How's guidance-counseloring?" to Mr. Rosenberg, our guidance counselor.

For some reason, even though I feel like crying, I laugh. I just completely crack up. And everyone in homeroom turns to look at me. Then they notice what I'm looking at, and they start laughing. Laughing at me? With me? Both, I guess.

"You have to laugh at yourself," I say. "Right, guys? Right?"

Then they stop laughing and give me that pointy-eyed, you're-very-strange look.

"What's gotten into you all?" Mrs. Welsh calls from her desk. "This is way, way too loud."

Lee shakes her head. "They'll forget about it soon. Just scroll down, you can see the other terrible things that have been posted on the page."

The thing is, I appreciate a good joke. And it was just a video of me falling, not throwing up on someone or losing bladder control or something. But what bothers me is who posted it.

Three names: Kendall, Molly, and Chelsea.

Obviously, only one of them actually posted it, most definitely Kendall, the first one listed. But the two others totally went along with it. And that's the worst part. One person could have said, "Oh, don't do that."

But she didn't. That's the problem.

As I'm walking to science, clutching my backpack and

trying to avoid being chipped again, I see Ross and his whole group of boys outside the gym.

Ross sees me and then shushes all the boys, and then they all look up and stare at me.

Is this video really so scandalous? I don't get it. Is it so interesting that everyone has to talk about it and then stare at me as I walk by?

I put my head down and keep walking, around the corner, past the locker rooms.

And then I hear my name.

"Dina Gross?" one of the boys asks.

"Dude," another one says. "That video . . ."

"Oh, come on, that was so stupid. Kendall trying to keep her reign over everyone." Silence. "Dina's chill."

A voice mumbles, "Grunny . . ."

"Whatever. You guys are just jealous you didn't notice her first," I hear that same someone say. It's Ross. He has the deepest voice out of all of them. "She's cute, and totally, like, normal."

Ross is talking about me. And saying good things.

Anywhere but here "normal" would be a synonym for boring. But in Rockwood Hills, normal's actually kind of unusual. Unique, even. We're living in some alternate universe.

I keep walking.

Ross Grunner likes me.

Ross Grunner: a popular, cute boy who wears real shoes to school instead of sneakers, and whose jeans always look ironed.

That Ross Grunner. Likes me.

They were talking about the video, but they were talking about more than that, too. Ross was saying that he likes me.

I say that over and over in my head a billion times, and then I remember that I have to find Chelsea so we can work on the project. Because who knows what will happen with the Ross Grunner thing. His friends will probably convince him I'm lame and not cool . . . But I still can't help being excited.

And besides, none of that matters, because Chelsea and I still have to finish this project.

I have just enough time to find Chelsea before the bell rings. We'll talk about the project, and then I'll just come out and ask her why she did what she did.

I'll put her on the spot, get it out in the open.

My mind snaps back and forth between Ross and finding Chelsea, and it feels like I'm in a cartoon where the character falls and hits his head and all those spirals are circling around.

Except I haven't fallen. Not since the time when it was videoed.

I can't find Chelsea, and the bell rings. I have to go to science.

When I get to class and I'm waiting for it to start, I start to wonder: Did I just imagine that Ross Grunner thing? Is this a dream? Am I still asleep in my bed?

It's all so crazy—good crazy and bad crazy at the same time.

26

CHELSEA

Sasha Preston piece of advice: If you're feeling nervous, make eye contact. It makes things easier.

"So?"

I'm at Dina's lunch table. I said I'd come here to discuss the project, but she's looking at me like she doesn't know why I'm even here. Even though the cute kid who helps in the library sits a table away, I don't really want to be here, either, taking my precious lunchtime to work on the project. I should be back at my own lunch table, making my friends realize that I'm still cool, still the old Chelsea.

No one at this table is really talking; they're all just sitting there studying with books on their laps. They don't even take a break to eat lunch.

"So what are your ideas?" I ask Dina. "We really have to get this done, you know."

I don't mean to sound rude, but I feel awkward standing here. And we've been going around and around in circles about this for weeks.

Dina takes her last bite of peanut butter and jelly sandwich. Katherine, Maura, Trisha, and the other girls at the table barely look at her; that's how hard they're studying. Then her chair makes an awful squeaking sound against the hideous linoleum floor, and everyone looks up, staring at me. I smile but don't say anything. I wonder if Trisha's thinking what I'm thinking, remembering the time I went into the city with her family when we were in third grade. Her dad even paid for us to go on a horse and buggy ride. It was pretty awesome.

I start to wonder what life would be like if I had stayed friends with Trisha, if Trisha was a part of our group. In third grade, you can be friends with anyone. It's just not like that now, even though I'm sure everyone wishes it was.

As we leave, Dina doesn't say good-bye to the table, which is weird. This whole thing is weird. Who even knew this awkwardness took place on the other side of the cafeteria?

"Come with me," Dina says. I follow her. I'd follow her anywhere if she'd make this stupid project go away.

We stop in the hall outside the cafeteria. The juice and water machine is buzzing softly next to us. I lean up against it because I feel too tired to stand up at the moment, and the coolness feels good against my cheek. My dad has no job; Ross likes Dina. How did this become my life?

"You have the camera, right?" I ask.

She nods.

Every time I look at Dina, all I think about is the Ross thing. I try to put it out of my head, but I can't. If I just pretend the situation doesn't exist, maybe it will actually go away. I don't care what I promised Ross. She has no idea he likes her, and I plan on keeping it that way. I doubt he'll ever really do anything about it on his own.

She's wearing her usual not-baggy-but-not-tight-either jeans and a red zip-up sweater. And I look at her closely because I'm trying to tell if she's pretty. I mean, I know she's not hideously ugly, but I'm not sure I'd describe her as pretty.

I try to figure out what Ross sees in her. I don't know why him liking her bothers me, since I didn't even like him in the first place, but it does.

"Can I just talk to you for a sec?" she asks. "About something that's not the project."

The way she asks I can tell it's something she's been thinking about saying, and that makes me nervous.

"I'm just gonna come out and say this," she starts.

That's never a good sign.

"The other day," she goes on, "Kendall was talking about Gatsby's and the plans for your birthday dinner. And, um, am I invited?"

Did she just ask what I thought she asked? I don't understand how she can just ask to be invited to something. That's, like, a universal rule, something you just don't do. Plus it's a little ridiculous that it's the first thing on her mind at the moment.

And then I remember the video Kendall posted. Has she seen it yet? Should I tell her about it before she sees it?

But the truth is, Dina being invited to my party doesn't even matter because I have to tell Kendall to cancel it anyway. My parents can't afford to pay for a big, fancy birthday dinner, and I don't want to make them feel bad about that.

"Um, well, see, Kendall made the plans," I say. I don't want to hurt her feelings, but what can I say? I see Dina's face sinking. "And so I didn't plan it at all, and I didn't make the guest list. And I'm on thin ice with them, actually. Things are weird with us." I pause and wait for her to tell me she understands, but she doesn't. "The party probably won't even happen, anyway, though."

Dina's head snaps back like she's just heard the craziest thing ever. "You're on thin ice with them? They're your best friends. Why? And why isn't it going to happen?"

"I can't say. But I'm really sorry."

Dina says, "I don't understand: are we friends or not? Just tell me."

"We're not friends," I say before I have a chance to think about it. I feel bad after I say it, but I'm so mad about everything that the feeling-bad thing just sort of fades into the background. "Okay? We're just working on a project together, and we were forced to pair up. And I'm sorry you have no friends here, but that's not my fault. And I just don't have the time to deal with any of this."

Dina walks away from me, which is not surprising. Then she turns around and says, "Well, I'm glad that I know the truth now. I feel better. I didn't think we were friends, since you posted that video or let your stupid friends post that video. And you didn't tell me about your dad getting fired, or that Ross Grunner likes me and not you. So I doubted it. But now I know for sure."

She says it so loud that I immediately look around to make sure no one else is in the hallway. I'm relieved that it's empty.

She knows about Ross.

She knows about about my dad. She's a detective.

"Sorry if that's too much for you to deal with now, too." She runs down the stairs and leaves me standing alone by the vending machines.

It's one of those things that replays over and over again in your head, but you don't really believe that it happened. That's kind of how it was when my dad first lost his job, too. It's like my brain knew it happened, but I couldn't believe it. I kept thinking it wasn't true, that I had somehow made it up.

It isn't made up, though. It's all true.

I get home from school, and the first thing my mom says is, "I thought you were staying after school to work on the video."

"Change of plans." I end the conversation right there and go up to my room.

I may not be friends with Dina, and she may be a stalker, but I still don't like the fact that the video is up on the Internet. I want to take it down and delete the comments.

But the video won't let me. Kendall posted it, so she needs to delete it.

"Take down the video," I tell her over the phone.

"Why?" She laughs. "Come on, it was funny. You said it yourself. You can't seriously feel bad about it. No one's, like, abusing the girl or anything."

"Just take it down, Ken," I snap. "There's such a thing as cyber-bullying, you know. Remember the assembly?"

"Oh, come on, no one takes that seriously," she huffs.

"Yes, they do," I say. "Just take it down. Now."

She's eating something, and it sounds so loud over the

phone. In between bites, she says, "If you want to be friends with new girl, then go ahead, but don't be friends with us anymore."

It sounds so unbelievably ridiculous that I can't even take it seriously. It's like saying if you eat sushi, you can't eat pizza or something. "Are you serious?"

"Yup."

I swivel around in my desk chair trying to think of what I can say to her to make her take the video down and to make her stop being so impossible. "You're jealous, Ken. That's it. You're jealous that I'm hanging out with someone besides you."

"What did you just say?" she asks.

"I said you're jealous. You always want what everyone else has, and you're always jealous. Just admit it. And stop being that way."

Kendall laughs her obnoxious, annoying laugh. "Yeah. I'm really jealous of you, Chelsea. Because your life is just soooo awesome." She snickers. "Your perfect little world isn't so perfect anymore. You're poor, and the boy you like likes someone else. And everyone knows." She stops talking for a second. "Everyone knows everything."

27

DINA

Video tip: Sometimes it helps to ask an interviewee
to restate the question in the answer.

"So, we're not friends," I tell Ali on the phone as I'm scrolling through all the extra footage I got after school. By myself. Chelsea and I are not at all close to finishing the project, but at least we're taking baby steps. Well, I'm taking baby steps. I'm the one who's doing all the work. "You would have been so proud of me. I just came out and asked her if I could go to her birthday dinner."

"You did?"

"Yeah. What's wrong with that?"

"Sorry, but that's kind of nuts," she says. "I mean, I know you're gutsy and you'll do anything, but that crosses a line."

"Thanks." I'm only half-listening to what Ali's saying because it's kind of hurting my feelings and because I'm working on the video at the same time. The beginning is going to be all the scenery shots of the school but played at ultra-fast speed, and then it will slow down when I introduce the individual shots of the kids.

"I'm just being honest. Aren't we supposed to be honest with each other?" Ali asks.

"I guess." I scroll through more footage. "And I didn't tell you—one of her friends posted this video of me falling. It's been an awesome week around here."

She cracks up. "Oh, man. You *are* kind of a klutz. What about the video you're making? Did you finish it?"

"Ha!" I yell. "Yeah, right. We barely even started it." I move my phone away from my ear so I can see who is beeping on the other line. "Oh, can I call you back? I'm getting another call."

"Who's calling you? Your grandma? I thought you don't have any friends there."

"No idea, but I should get it." That's a lie; I know who it is. It's Ross. But I can't tell Ali that. She'd freak out. She's never had a boy call her, or a boy like her, or anything. Neither have I, up until now, but I don't want to make her feel bad. And if I can't even tell her that he's calling, how can I tell her that he likes me?

"Bye," she says.

She sounds annoyed, but there's nothing I can do about

it. We haven't been talking that much lately. I've been so preoccupied with Sasha Preston and Chelsea and all of that stuff, I haven't really had time to miss her.

"Dina?" Ross says after I say hello. I pinch my arm to make sure this is actually happening. There's a boy's voice on the other end of the line. And it's a boy who likes me. And a boy who's actually cool, and cute, and easy to talk to.

I sit back in my bed, my pillows propped up behind me. I feel like Sasha Preston on her show, because that's how she ends every episode. The only thing that could ruin this is if my dad knocks on the door right now and asks me who I'm talking to.

"Hi," I say. "Are you calling to tell me how hilarious that video of me falling was?"

He laughs. "No. I called to see what you thought of the English essay today," he answers, like it was the only thing he could think to say.

"Easy," I say. "I'm actually kind of good at English."

"Well your comments about *To Kill a Mockingbird* were very astute." He laughs. He's fully quoting our English teacher Mrs. Einsel.

"Thank you. I'm often called astute." I laugh and then he laughs again, and I'm not even totally sure what we're laughing about. But it feels good to laugh. Especially after what happened with the video and then with Chelsea today.

"So, I never even got to ask you—how do you like Rockwood Hills so far?"

"Um, take a guess." He doesn't say anything so I blurt out, "I hate it. Sorry. No offense."

I don't feel bad that I said that, because I really do hate it. And I don't think anyone's given me any reason to like it really.

Well, up until now. Ross calling me is making me like it a tiny bit more. And the fact that he likes me enough to call—okay, that's pretty great. But I can't say that. I can't say he's the reason why I don't want to put Rockwood Hills in the *Guinness Book of World Records* for the worst town ever.

"I'm not offended. I'm not the mayor or anything."

"You seem to like it here, though," I tell him. "So maybe you can give me some pointers." I don't even say this to be flirty, but after I say it, I realize that it sounds that way.

"Hang out with me," he says. "If you want to."

"That's the secret to liking this town?" I ask. In my head, I'm making a list of all the things I will want to tell Ali about this conversation if I get up the courage to actually tell her about it.

"It's a start," he says. "We can study for the social studies test together if you want."

That was one of the things Ali and I daydreamed would

happen after I moved here. Me, studying with a boy. Such a teenager thing to do. And now it's actually happening. Maybe it's one of those things—like, I can't have the friends and the boy at the same time. You can't always have it all. Now that I know for sure I don't have the friends, I guess I can have the boy.

"Okay," I say. "Where should we study?"

"Come to my house after school tomorrow," he says. "Or do you have to work with Chelsea on the project?"

"I'm not sure. It's confusing." I pause, wondering if that sounds weird. "But I can skip a day."

"Great," he says, and he sounds really happy. "Well, I'll see you in school tomorrow."

We hang up. I replay the conversation over and over again in my head. I can't believe it just happened. And I know that people say all the time that they can't believe that things just happened. But when I say this now, I really can't believe it.

I text Ali because it's after nine, which is too late to call her house.

> just talked to that boy on the phone. we r studying together 2morrow.

It takes Ali eleven minutes to respond, which is so not like her. She is usually such a fast texter.

> wow. Sleeping now. Talk tomorrow.

That's it? Just "wow" and no exclamation points or anything?

After all that, I can't fall asleep. I can't stop thinking about Ali saying it was weird for me to just come out and ask about Chelsea's birthday party. And then I think about the video of me falling, and then Ross calling. And I hear Chelsea saying we're not friends over and over in the background. There's too much to think about.

And then I remember the project.

I spend another hour looking through the footage I have, moving things around, playing with the Sasha footage.

It's not enough. It's not right. And Chelsea's no help.

I decide to e-mail Sasha. She told us we could, but we had to promise not to give her e-mail address to anyone else. I can be trusted, but I don't know about Chelsea.

Dear Sasha,

The fiftieth-anniversary gala is coming up, and we still haven't really figured out what to do for the video. I know you said to observe and try to catch people doing their thing, trying to really show the people of the school. But it seems boring. Do you have any other ideas? I don't have any other help—Chelsea's really not my friend, she said so herself. And her friends totally hate me—they posted a video online of me falling in the hallway. So I really need your help. Just pretend I'm a character on the show and you're you. Maybe something will come to you.

Thanks so much,

Dina

At lunch the next day, the Acceptables are stressing out over their math test. They calculate their averages at least ten times, figuring out what they'll be if they score high on the test (for them, 100) or low on the test (for them, 90).

I'm just glad they're not discussing Chelsea and Ross. Because I really don't know what to say about either of them at the moment.

"So, you guys," I start. "I still have so much work to do on this video. Do any of you have ideas? You've been at Rockwood Hills for way longer than I have."

They all stare at me.

"Well, since you met Sasha Preston, you could have her act something out," Katherine says. "People would be really impressed."

I think about that for a second. It could work, I guess, but it doesn't seem totally right. "Do you mind if I shoot you guys eating lunch?"

"No!" Trisha screams. She's laughing, so I realize she's not really angry. "You can't tape us eating!"

"No way," Katherine says. "I don't want to be in it."

"My mom's really excited to meet you," Maura says, changing the subject. "She's glad there's someone new in the group."

Even though I don't totally love the Acceptables, because they're just, well, acceptable, I'm glad to hear I'm in the group, that they consider me a part of the group.

"I'm excited, too," I say, and it surprises me, but I actually mean that.

I was fighting so hard to be friends with Chelsea and Kendall and all of them, but I just don't feel like fighting anymore. It's just not worth it. They really don't like me. They proved that with the video, and with Chelsea's speech to me the other day. Fighting to be friends with someone who doesn't like you, who doesn't even tolerate you, seems pointless.

Maybe the Acceptables are more than acceptable. Maybe they'll end up being the Preferables.

28

CHELSEA

Sasha Preston piece of advice: Put yourself in
the other person's place. If you want an apology,
then they want one, too.

As I'm leaving the cafeteria, Dina and I literally bump
into each other, which doesn't bother me so much because I have
to talk to her about the project anyway, and also because part of
me wants to smack her. She's hanging out with Ross after school,
and he just told my whole lunch table about it. It kind of seems
like he's rebelling against something, but I don't know what.

"We have to finish the video," I tell her. "Should we meet
today after school?"

I'm doing this to test her, because I want to see what
she's going to say. I wonder if she'll bail on Ross to work on
the video or if she'll tell me about Ross. I wonder if she even

knows that I was the one who was supposed to be going out with Ross, not her.

"I can't. Tomorrow. Okay?"

"Fine." I walk away without saying anything else.

But then I feel guilty about it, and also really stupid about the way I'm acting. I'm not going to keep up this hostility with her. If she's going to go out with Ross Grunner, then I want to know every detail about it. I want to know the details that he doesn't give me. And if she's going to know all this stuff about my family anyway, then I want to know how and why she knows and if she's telling people about it.

I think this is a case of "Keep your friends close, but keep your enemies closer." But I'm not sure, because I don't think I've ever had an enemy before. Anyway, Dina doesn't feel like an enemy. Not all the time.

I'm going to take a totally different approach with her, starting tomorrow.

When I get home from school, my parents are sitting in the den, talking. They're not yelling at each other; they're actually talking, and sipping coffee from Dunkin' Donuts.

"Honey, we want to talk to you," my mom says.

I hesitate but go in there and sit down next to her.

"We know this situation is hard for you," she says. "You're handling everything really well, though."

"Thanks." If she only knew everything that's been going on, I doubt she'd say that.

"Everything's going to be okay. You know that, right?" my dad asks.

There have been many times in my life when I felt like I was living in some sort of alternate after-school-special kind of universe, but I've never felt that way more than I'm feeling it right now. I nod. The past six months feel like they're piling up in my brain, and I'm afraid that I'll start to cry any minute. This is actually a rare occasion when my parents seem to be in a happy mood, and I can't ruin it with my tears. I need to hold it together. "I know." I smile and then get up from the couch. "I'm going to do homework now."

I check my e-mail when I get upstairs to my room and I see that I have an e-mail from Dina. It's a forward, and the subject line says "Any Advice?"

I open it, and there's a note at the top from Dina: "Asked Sasha for advice on the video since we had no clue. Here's what she said. Dina."

So I scroll down a little and see the note from Sasha. It's still really hard to believe Sasha's e-mailing us—or e-mailing Dina, really. I have her e-mail address on a piece of paper in my room, but I never would've just e-mailed her like Dina did.

Hey Dina,

Good to hear from you. At first I thought it would be good for you to be in the background, trying to film real life at Rockwood Hills Middle School. But now here's what I think: go around and actually talk to the kids at school, see what they think about stuff. Ask them questions and let them ramble on and then watch the footage all together and see what you can take from it. Sometimes if you really listen to what people are saying, you get ideas. Sometimes you have to ask tough questions to get good answers. Let me know how it goes.

Good luck!
Sasha

I e-mail Dina back.

Hi Dina,

This sounds like a good idea. I bet a lot of people at our school have stuff to say and just keep quiet because they're not sure if they should say it or not. Do you know what I mean? I bet everyone thinks I'm in love with things here. And I'm not. Let's meet in the library and see how we can set up real, actual interviews. See you tomorrow.

Chelsea

P.S. Sorry about the video. I didn't post it but I probably could've done more to get them to take it down sooner.

It's so much easier to be honest in an e-mail or a text or an IM, and it's so much easier to write things down than to say them out loud. Now that I've written that, I feel relieved, calmer—relaxed, even. I feel like I can stop hiding things and be honest and maybe Dina will understand.

The next day, Dina and I spend all of lunch making posters that say we want to interview people for the fiftieth anniversary and then putting them up around school. I keep thinking that the library helper will see us and ask about it and maybe even be interviewed. It's kind of crazy we've been working in the library for so long but we haven't talked at all.

Dina doesn't say anything about the e-mail, or that she's

forgiven me and that everything's okay again. She pretty much just puts up the posters quietly and doesn't talk.

And then after school, she comes running into the library five minutes late, which is so not like her.

"I came up with questions," she starts, not even saying hello or how are you or any of the customary greetings.

"Let me see," I say.

She hands me the sheet. It's all typed up and everything.

Tell us your honest thoughts about Rockwood Hills Middle School.

How do you feel about being chipped? Or about chipping others?

Do you feel like you are accepted for who you are?

What are the strengths of the school? The weaknesses?

How can we improve Rockwood Hills for the future?

When you think of Rockwood Hills Middle School, what's the first thing that comes to mind?

What's something that's unique about you?

"Good questions," I tell her, not because I want to compliment her but because I really do think they're good.

"Thanks." She smiles. "Sasha said if we ask the tough questions, we'll get good answers. So that's what I'm doing. By the way, why weren't you in social studies today?"

"I had to do that physical-fitness-profile thing because I was absent the day we did it in gym. Why?"

Dina sits back in her chair. "Mr. Valakis is a little worried we haven't shown him any footage yet," she says. "I said we're just getting it all together, and we'd show him as soon as possible."

"Did he buy it?" I ask.

She shrugs. "Not sure. You're probably going to have to talk to him."

"What do you mean?" I ask. I kind of hate how she's totally taking charge right now, and telling me what to do. I said I was sorry in that e-mail. Why isn't she happy?

"Well, just explain to him what's been taking so long."

Dina never would've bossed me around like this before. I want the old Dina back. Maybe I took her for granted. "Fine. Whatever you say. We're probably not gonna get any people to interview today," I tell her, "since we just put up the signs."

"So we'll start the interviews tomorrow," she says.

Dina's still totally giving me the cold shoulder, and I guess I understand why, even though I don't like it.

"No one's just gonna be interviewed by you guys and then have it shown in front of a million people at the gala," someone says from the table next to us. Apparently, he's been listening to our conversation. "You know that, right?"

We turn around to see who it is. It's Damien Chiu. He's in my math class. He sits with the video-game boys, the ones who try to sneak their DSs into the cafeteria. He has round glasses and a red polo shirt, and his arms are all chapped from dry skin. I should recommend lotion, but I won't.

"Why?" Dina asks. "It's not like you have to reveal anything that personal."

He shrugs and goes back to his books. "That's just my opinion."

"Do you think that's true?" Dina asks me. "Are we totally doing the wrong thing? I mean, Sasha said to do this. She knows what she's talking about."

"What if we tell people we'll block out their faces, like in those spooky interviews on TV when people don't want other people to know who they are?" I suggest.

"That would be hard to watch," Dina says. "But good idea." She smiles, and maybe she's softening up to me. "But we'll just tell people we're not going to go around sharing anything they don't want to share."

Nobody comes. We just sit there and sit there and sit there.

"Well, maybe people have already gone home today," Dina says. "It is the end of the day."

I nod. Maybe she's right. There are so many things I want to bring up right now, but I don't bring up any of them. I don't ask her about Ross and I don't mention the video or my birthday party or anything. I want to bring them up, but I'm just not sure the best way to do it.

"I bet we'll have a ton of interviews tomorrow," I tell Dina, trying to cheer her up. She looks defeated.

I look at the poster again.

COME BE INTERVIEWED FOR THE "DAY IN THE LIFE OF A ROCKWOOD HILLS STUDENT" VIDEO! IT WILL BE SHOWN AT THE GALA! MEET IN THE LIBRARY AFTER SCHOOL UNTIL 5 P.M.!

"I have an idea!" I yell, and I'm actually beyond excited, because it's the first time in this whole process that I've even had a single good idea. "This poster makes it sound boring! We need to make it more exciting. We need to prove that there's something in it for them."

"Free food?" Dina laughs. "I could have my mom bring in pizza."

I crack up. Dina's answer to everything is food, and it's hilarious. "Good idea, but no. Why don't we say something like, 'Speak your mind about Rockwood Hills. Share an insider's opinion on the school. Be a reality star at the gala! Real life—starring you!'? Stuff like that!"

Dina smiles her closed-mouth smile. "I like it, but do you think people will go for it? Will they actually say anything we can use?"

"I think so," I tell her. "It makes it sound exciting, a chance to make a name for themselves. A chance for them to speak their minds. That's what Sasha says people want, right?"

Dina agrees after a few minutes more of convincing, and we make new posters. We take the other ones down and recycle the paper and then hang the new ones up.

"I think we're getting somewhere," I tell Dina as we're waiting for our moms in the parking lot. "Finally."

"I hope so," she says.

Dina's mom gets there before my mom does, and as I'm

waiting, I wonder more and more about the interviews, if people will really be honest. But I think it's all about the fact that people do want to be reality stars, and they want to be reality stars because they want to be remembered. I mean, that's the whole thing with Facebook, and documenting everything, right? Why else would people share every photo, every update, every video?

They want to be remembered, they want to be seen.

It's the same thing here.

29

DINA

Video tip: Make your subject feel at ease
and you'll get better footage.

Everyone's talking about our posters the next day.
The new and improved posters, that is.

People stop to look at them in the hallway. Even Mr. Valakis comes up to us after class to discuss them. "So you're interviewing all the students?" he asks. "Interesting idea."

"And fun!" I add. "This way everyone's getting to be a star."

"Well, remember it has to be five minutes," he says. "We can't have this video be hours long. You girls have been quite secretive about this whole thing, and it's going to be very exciting to see it up on the big screen."

"It totally will be," Chelsea says.

• • •

We're in the library after school, and there's a line of people waiting to be interviewed. A real line!

"Okay, guys, we'll be calling you up one by one," Chelsea yells out to everyone. Mr. Singer is behind the circulation desk, and he looks a little nervous, probably about all the noise.

"What? You're the one doing this?" a girl yells at Chelsea. "We can't say what we want to say in front of *you*."

Chelsea just stands there.

"*You* think everything's perfect here! We can't speak our mind."

"Calm down, it's okay." I try to smooth things over, but instead everyone just gets more riled up.

"Yeah, little miss perfect life Chelsea Stern," another girl says.

"Forget it—let's go," people start saying.

"No, no, it's okay." I stand in front of the door to try to get them to stay. We're running out of time, and this was our last idea. But it was our best idea. They should realize that by participating they're going to be a part of something big, something important, something that people will probably be watching for years and years to come.

"No, this is lame. Come on guys, let's go," a boy says.

"That's what you guys really think?" Chelsea yells. "That my life is perfect all the time? That I love it here?"

Everyone stops. No one says anything.

"Well, I don't. I mean, I love it sometimes. But it's not perfect. I feel like an outsider even with my own friends. You guys all seem to hate me. Things aren't always so easy at my house." She stops talking suddenly. Everyone's listening intently. "It's not perfect. Things are not always the way they seem."

People remain quiet. I just look at Chelsea. I wonder how she feels after saying that. I wonder if she feels better. I wonder if everyone will see her differently now.

Only a few people leave; most stay and wait for the interviews.

Our first interviewee is a tall, lanky girl with long hair. I don't know her, and obviously Chelsea has never spoken to this girl in her life.

"So where should I start?" she asks.

I have the camera in my hand, and I'm ready to hit Record. "Anywhere you want."

"Well, first of all, I can't believe that *you*"—she looks at Chelsea—"would even care to hear what other people think of the school. I'm surprised you're not just making this video of your own little friends."

Chelsea stays quiet. Was this girl not listening when Chelsea gave that whole speech a few minutes ago?

"Delete that from the video," the girl says. "I just had to get it off my chest."

I nod. "Let's just start with your name and something interesting about yourself."

"Interesting? Something I find interesting or something you guys would find interesting?" She crosses and uncrosses her legs, and leans back in the chair.

"Either," I say.

"Well, I'm Christine Whitmore. And, um, I collect T-shirts. I have over four hundred T-shirts." She laughs. "But that's probably not interesting. They're not cool; no one here thinks they're cool."

I keep recording, and she goes on and on. "No one likes me here. Can that be in the video? People treat me like I'm some kind of freak because I don't play tennis and buy fancy clothes." She goes on and on about all the ways she feels excluded and ostracized and then she says, "Happy anniversary, Rockwood Hills. This school's awful." She gets up and walks away.

"She's always been so crazy," Chelsea says. "Now she's even crazier! That was just a whole bunch of whining."

"I don't know if she's crazy," I say. "But it was whining."

After that Kendall and Molly come skipping in, and they don't even acknowledge me except to ask me if the camera's on and if I'm ready to tape them.

"We're total stars," Molly says. "You're gonna thank us for making your video so awesome."

"Um, hmm," I mumble. I can't believe I wanted to be friends with these people so badly. Worse than that is that I can't believe I still kind of do. But they're happy. They like it here. So why wouldn't I want to be a part of that?

That's what this is all about. That's what being popular is. The popular people seem happy, and so everyone wants to be friends with them. But if Chelsea's like the rest of them, it's all an act. Maybe none of them are as happy as they seem.

"Just go," Chelsea says. I've never seen her act this way around them before. It's like she doesn't even care that they're here. She's not making eye contact with them. I wonder if they got into a fight.

I tell them to say their names and an interesting fact about themselves, because after Christine the T-shirt hoarder, I think it's a good way to get each clip started.

"I'm Kendall. I love shopping."

Boring.

"I'm Molly. I collect shoes."

Boring.

They go on and on about how Rockwood Hills is so great, how they love each other and the school.

But I don't know if I buy it.

And then after that it's interview after interview after interview of whining.

"Everyone thinks I'm a dork because I want to start a mathletes team," this kid Keith says. "But I like math—that's the interesting thing about myself. I actually like math."

Chelsea cracks up at that, which makes me crack up. I realize this is the exact opposite of how we're supposed to respond to a comment like that. But it's just funny, the way he says it.

"My dad's a pilot, for people's private planes. And I've met tons of famous people. But yet I'm known as the bloody-nose kid, just because I got bloody noses in fourth grade," this kid Jordan says.

Sophia from my gym class goes on and on about how she likes to knit, and how in other places knitting is cool.

Even the Acceptables come in. They said they didn't want to be part of it, but I guess they do now.

"The thing about this place is that everyone wants to be like everyone else," Maura says, and I think she's onto something. "That's just how it is. So no one wants to stand out."

And we ask them how we can make the school better, what we could do, what everyone could do.

"If everybody could just be who they are and not worry

about it, it would be better," this girl Abby Howard says. "Maybe that's cheesy and lame, but it's true."

Finally, we're done with all the interviews. I'm tired and overwhelmed. Chelsea looks the same way. Her head's down on the table.

"I guess it's up to us to figure out what to do with all of this, how to turn it into something good," I say. "We can't just show this raw footage."

Chelsea sighs. "Yeah, you're right."

I text Ross to tell him I'll be over soon to study, and Chelsea reads the text over my shoulder.

"You're hanging out with Ross again?" she asks, sounding more sad than angry.

"We're just studying."

Chelsea and I walk out to the parking lot together. "I'll probably spend the whole time thinking about how to get this video done, anyway," I say.

I say good-bye to Chelsea and find my dad's car. He was working from home today, so he's going to drop me off at Ross's house.

"Who's this Ross kid?" he asks.

"Just a person." I smile.

"Just a person?" my dad mimics. "A little more info, please."

"I don't know!" I yell. "He's a kid in my grade, Dad. What?"

He shakes his head. "Fine, don't tell me anything."

I get to Ross's house and his housekeeper lets me in. I feel really bad that I've forgotten her name, but I was only at his house one other time. I just smile and say hello.

"Ross is upstairs," she says.

Did he not hear the doorbell ring? Now I have to walk all the way up the twisty staircase by myself. And I don't know where his room is up there. I could be wandering around lost for a while—his house is really big.

He should be here to greet me.

And I'm not sure that I want to be alone with him in his room.

I tiptoe up the spiral staircase, but I don't know why I'm tiptoeing. It's late afternoon, not three in the morning or something.

I hear a door open as I'm walking up. Oh, please don't let it be his mom. Or his dad. That would be even worse.

"Dina?" I hear. It's Ross. "I thought I heard something."

He's already changed out of what he was wearing at school—dark fancy jeans with a gray thermal. He's the only boy I know who can make a thermal look dressed up. Now he's wearing blue shorts and a Yankees T-shirt.

I wonder if I should tell him now or later that I'm a Red Sox fan. I wonder if he'll care that we're supposed to be big rivals.

"Come in, I'm typing up a study sheet," he says.

I'm not sure if I'm ready to be alone in a boy's room. That may be pathetic since I'm in eighth grade, but I can't help it. It makes me nervous.

He sits on his bed, and I sit in the swivel desk chair. His room is really neat—way too neat for a boy's. Not that I've ever been in a boy's room before.

"Tell me about the New Deal," he says.

So I do. I tell him all about President Franklin Delano Roosevelt and how he wanted to get things back on track during the Great Depression and how he started the fireside chats and all the new programs. I tell him that FDR is my favorite president.

"You have a favorite president?" he says, like I just told him I had a favorite brand of garbage bags, something no one would care about.

"Yeah. Don't you?"

"No. Never thought about it." He laughs.

He keeps quizzing me on history, and I'm surprising myself with how much I know. I haven't even really started studying yet. I figured I'd officially start this weekend. If the

Acceptables haven't started yet, then I didn't need to, either. That's what I told myself.

We finish the end of the study sheet, and we pretty much covered everything.

"So, what are you doing this weekend?" he asks me.

I wonder if I should lie. Saying I'm hanging out with Maura, Katherine, and Trisha probably seems kind of sad to someone like Ross.

"Just hanging out," I say.

"Cool. Do you need any more interviews for the video, by the way?"

"Maybe. I mean, we need as much footage as we can get. And what we have—well, we can't use all of it."

He gives me a confused look. "Why not?"

"It's a lot of whining," I say. "I don't really love the school or anything, but we can't just show people complaining. No one likes that."

"Well, did you get different opinions and angles and stuff?"

"I guess. The cool part is that we had each kid say something interesting about themselves at the beginning. Everyone does really unique and cool stuff that no one even knows about."

"So show that," he says, rubbing his thumb against the pages in the textbook.

That's an idea, actually. That shows our differences, our

unique qualities. It shows we're all different and all have something to offer and should all be accepted.

"I think you just solved the problem! And if I know what we're doing, I can get started on what I'm most excited about—the editing. That's my specialty."

"Really." He says it like a statement, like he doesn't believe me.

"What?" I smile. "I'm telling the truth."

"iMovie or Final Cut?" he asks, like he still doesn't believe me.

"Final Cut," I tell him.

"I'm amazing at iMovie," he says. "But I'd love to learn Final Cut. Maybe I could help?"

"Really?" I smile. "You're, like, into this stuff?"

"Totally." He pats his bed to get me to come sit next to him. It's a little embarrassing—that's how you'd get a dog to come over to you. But I don't think about it too much. He opens his laptop and starts playing some clips.

"You shot these?" I ask. I'm sitting so close to him now, too close. I finally understand that expression *too close for comfort*. I want to inch away, but then I won't be able to see the clips.

He nods. They're just random shots of places around Rockwood Hills, but they have a cool, artsy look to them. They zoom in on simple details, and the shots of people are all really emotional and expressive. And he put all this music in the background that fits with the shots perfectly.

"You just do this for fun?"

"Yup."

"Why didn't you say anything sooner? I mean, we have so much in common, and you knew Chelsea and I were working on this film project . . ."

"Chelsea and I . . ." His voice sort of trails off. "We don't really get along that great anymore."

"Yeah. What's up with that?" I ask. I know I'm being nosy. I know it's not really my business. But I *am* sitting with Ross Grunner, on his bed, on his green-and-beige plaid comforter with his Yankee prints all over the wall. When you get that close to someone—like, in their space—maybe things like that do become your business.

"She thought I liked her." He keeps fiddling with his computer. It's like he can't look at me.

"And?"

"I do like her. Just not like that."

"Oh." Now I can't look at him, either.

"Dina," he says.

"Yeah." I still can't look at him.

"It's because I like you."

I feel his eyes on me, and I finally look up and every bit of excitement I felt about Ross before is now suddenly gone. All I feel is scared. More scared than I've been in my entire life.

"That's cool," I say, and laugh. I shouldn't laugh. It seems like I'm laughing at him, which I'm not. But it seems that way anyway, and I can't stop.

"That's cool?" he repeats, like he's shocked at my response.

"No one likes me here, so it's cool." I laugh again. I'm not the kind of person who always makes fun of herself. But for some reason it seems like it's the only normal way for me to act right now.

"Riiiiggghhht. Now you're the one whining." He raises his eyebrows, and then closes his computer. "Actually, I'm supposed to meet some of my boys for basketball, so I kind of have to go."

That can't be true. It has to be a lie to get me out of his house. Otherwise, he would have told me about the basketball sooner. I know I did something wrong. I should have said I liked him, too. But I'm not sure. I like that he likes me, though. Isn't that enough?

"Okay. Well, I can walk home from here," I tell him.

"Cool."

He walks me out, and I say thanks, and he tells me he thinks I'll do great on the test.

"I'll see you before the test," I remind him.

"Yeah, but, whatever. Just a vote of confidence."

I walk outside, and he closes the door behind me. I call Ali on my walk home, but she doesn't answer.

I feel like I messed up. But I don't even know what I wanted to happen. Or what I want to happen now.

But I really do want to work on the editing with him. I hope that offer still stands.

30

CHELSEA

Sasha Preston piece of advice: To ease brain freeze, hold your tongue to the roof of your mouth.

Kendall and Molly e-mailed me that we should meet at Starbucks and talk, face-to-face, about everything that's happened.

I'm just glad to be talking to them again. I've still been sitting with them at lunch, but at the end of the table, and I haven't been talking that much.

It's unseasonably warm for December, and we're sitting at one of the outside tables drinking lemonade iced tea.

"I guess I was just really upset that you didn't tell us," Kendall says, starting the conversation. I believe her—that she really was upset, and probably for the right reasons. Kendall sometimes makes me nervous, but underneath all of that, she does care.

"I felt like I couldn't," I say, shifting in my chair. "I knew it would make things weird between us, and it did."

"Because you didn't tell us," Molly jumps in, pushing her sunglasses to the top of her head.

"I'm sorry if I hurt you by keeping it from you," I admit. "That wasn't my plan. I was just feeling really bad about a million things."

They nod. "We hope you know we're here for you now," Molly says, and as the words are coming out of her mouth, I'm still not sure if I believe her. I guess I should try to, at least this time.

"But you guys acted so mean about the Dina thing," I say, and I'm proud of myself for being so honest. "I was just assigned to work with her, and I admit I wasn't happy about it at first, but you didn't need to be mean. You didn't need to accuse me of having a new friend and then leaving you guys, and you didn't need to post that video."

"We're sorry," Kendall says. "Honestly."

Molly nods as she's sipping her drink. "But we did take down the video."

"And for the record: I don't like Ross. I'm sorry to say that, but I don't. I wanted to, because it seemed like it would be the best thing, and you guys wanted me to like him. But I just don't."

I feel like I'm on some kind of reality show where the camera's on me and I have to make all these confessions, but it feels good to be doing this, to open up and be honest about everything for the first time.

They nod like they understand, but don't really know what to say to that.

I get a text, and since it's obviously not from Kendall or Molly, I look at my phone, excited to see who it's from.

Dina.

> Call when u can. I figured out the solution for the video. We're almost there!

I wonder what she means.

"Well, I guess the new girl doesn't like him, either. Did you hear about what happened between her and Ross?" Molly asks. She was probably reading the text over my shoulder. Either that or she just read my mind. But she knows her name is Dina—obviously she does, because she was instrumental in posting that video. Why can't she just say her name? After that whole conversation we just had, she should be able to say her name.

"No. What happened?" I ask after a brain-freeze-causing sip of my half-lemonade-half-iced-tea.

"She rejected him."

"Huh?" I ask. I find myself chewing on the end of my

straw. It grosses me out when I do that, but sometimes I can't help it.

"Apparently, he was all, like, I like you and stuff, and then she was, like, cool."

Kendall takes over the story. "And Ross is actually bummed. Or whatever. I mean, that's what Marcus said. So weird, right?"

"Maybe she didn't hear what he said," I tell them.

"Is she hard of hearing?" Kendall laughs. "Maybe she just doesn't like him. Maybe he can finally know what it's like to have someone not like him."

"She's not hard of hearing." I roll my eyes. "But she's, I don't know, like, innocent in that way. But really kind of cool."

"Cool how?" Molly asks. "Maybe if you'd just tell us, we'd understand, and we wouldn't feel so rejected. You hang out with her a lot. So just tell us what's so cool about her."

I try to think of the best way to explain this. "I don't know. Like, alternative? But not in like the hippie way. Like, a free-thinker? I can't explain it."

I hate when I can't explain things. And I hate when I say "like" a million times. Even I think I sound stupid.

"Well, it's gotta be something. Otherwise, Ross wouldn't like her." No one says anything after that, and I don't, either. We slurp our drinks, and I try not to think about Dina anymore. I want to call her right away and hear about the solution for the project, but I feel like it would be rude to just get up and call her and leave Molly and Kendall after our little heart-to-heart.

Molly says, "Maybe we should ask her to hang out tonight? She could tell us about the Ross thing. We can convince her to give him a chance."

"You're such a gossip, and an obvious one," Kendall says.

"So?" Molly looks at me like she thinks I'm going to agree with her. "Do you have her number, Chelsea? You must—you're working on the project together." Molly smiles and keeps chewing on the end of her straw. "Come on, it'll be fun. Like a new girl in the group. Not forever. Just for now. And I think Ross really does like her—maybe she just needs to be convinced by us a little that she should give him a chance."

She has that sneaky grin in her eyes, and I worry that I still can't trust her. I could never trust Molly. She has that sweet, innocent face, but her way of telling the truth can sound so mean.

"I'll call Dina," I say, relieved that I have an excuse to hear about the solution she's come up with. "But I don't know why in the world she'd want to hang out with you guys. You didn't even apologize for posting that terrible video."

"We'll say we're sorry tonight. But make sure she knows she's not sleeping over," Molly says. "That'd be too much. We don't know her well enough for that. Just invite her over for dinner and to hang out."

"Fine." I get up from the table and walk around the Starbucks a little. I don't want them overhearing my conversation.

Dina's cell phone rings three times and then goes straight to voice mail. I leave her a message to call me back because I'm dying to hear about her idea, and I also add that I'm wondering what she's up to tonight.

In a way I feel like a fairy godmother, since she's been wanting to hang out with me and my friends so badly. I wish I had been doing it all along.

31

DINA

Video tip: Never have your subject look directly
at the camera unless he or she is specifically
addressing the audience.

I get out of the shower and see that I have a missed call.
From Chelsea, of all people. She says she wants to hear about
my solution for the project, but she also wants to know what
I'm up to tonight.

Is this some kind of joke—something like the video of
me falling again? A prank? Maybe Ross is mad about the way
things ended before and he wants to play a trick on me.

I'm so paranoid for even thinking these things.

I get dressed, mostly because I want to stall calling her
back. Once my hair is dry, I decide to just take the plunge and
make the call.

"Hello?" she answers on the third ring.

There's noise in the background. She must be out somewhere.

"Hi, it's Dina," I say.

"Do you have plans tonight?" she asks.

I almost say no without even thinking about it because I'm so used to not having plans. But then I remember that I actually do have plans—with the Acceptables.

"Yeah," I say.

"Oh. Kendall, Molly, and I were wondering what you were up to," she says, and it sounds kind of like she's about to burst out laughing. "Well, what are you doing? I mean, maybe you can come hang out for, like, a little while." I hear voices in the background. It must be Kendall and Molly. They were talking about me? "By the way, they're sorry about the video."

The number of nights I wished for something like this to happen is too sad to mention. Like, every night before I went to bed. And now it's happening, and it feels off somehow. And I already have plans.

Things like this make me question my faith in the universe. I just don't get it. Why couldn't they have invited me over weeks ago, when I really needed them? Why couldn't they have invited me to the movies?

Why now? What changed?

"Oh, I'm actually going over to Maura's," I say and it feels sort of like being invited to meet the president but declining the invitation because you have to hang out with your cousin. And a cousin you don't even really like that much. But then I realize I'm excited to go to Maura's. She's not a cousin—she's a friend. I've been looking forward to it. I would much rather be with Maura and the Acceptables, who like me, than these girls.

Chelsea doesn't say anything for a few seconds. "So come before. When are you going over there?"

It seems like she's trying too hard. If I go over there, I'll probably get a bucket of water dumped on my head when I walk through the door. Or maybe I just watch too much television.

"Thanks, Chelsea, but I have plans," I say. "Have fun, though. I'll see you in school."

"Okay," she says. "Oh, and Dina?" She's almost whispering now, and it seems quieter in the background, like she moved away from where she was before.

"Yeah?"

"I'm sorry. Like, for being horrible pretty much the whole time we've been working together." She clears her throat.

"Okay."

"Do you forgive me?"

"I guess," I say. "You weren't that horrible." I laugh. "Well, you were just a little horrible."

Yeah, she told me we weren't friends. Yeah, she didn't stand up for me when her friends posted that video. But it's not like she threw food at me or embarrassed me in class. Or pulled my pants down in front of everyone. There are way worse things. "But forget about that for now!" I'm not sure how this conversation went on this long and we didn't discuss Ross's idea for the project. "I need to tell you about the idea, the solution to the video!"

"Oh, yeah! Tell!"

So I tell her about how Ross suggested that everyone could say one cool thing about themselves and then we could cut it together and make the faces and voices of Rockwood Hills.

"It sounds so perfect!" Chelsea says, and I can tell she means it. "By the way, you should call Ross."

"Huh?" I ask.

"He likes you, Dina." I wait for her to say more, but she doesn't.

I know that he likes me. I just don't really know what to do with that information. But that's too pathetic to admit.

"Just call him. Just to say hi. See what happens." She pauses. "And have fun tonight."

I hang up and go downstairs, where I find my mom and

my bubbie and her jokes club. They're always so happy to see me, and that feels good.

"Look at this beautiful girl," my bubbie says. "Have you ever seen someone so beautiful?"

She always says stuff like this, so I'm kind of used to it by now. And besides, it's one thing to hear your grandma tell you you're beautiful; it's another thing for a boy to say it or for the other girls at school to think you're pretty.

"The boys went bowling, so we decided to make it a girls' night," my mom says. I wonder if she gets depressed at the fact that she hangs out with women in their seventies. "Want to join us? We're having baked ziti."

"I have plans, Mom." I'm annoyed she didn't remember. This is a momentous occasion. And I'm not even dreading it. She should be more excited. "Remember?"

She nods, smiling, but trying to act that she's not way too excited.

When I get to Maura's, the Acceptables are all in the den eating tortilla chips and guacamole.

"We're not studying yet," Trisha says. "Obvs."

I laugh. "Okay, fine with me."

"Come sit." Katherine pats the couch. "We're watching some show about wedding planners to the staaaaaars."

I sit next to Katherine, and she passes me the bowl of chips and the bowl of guacamole.

"She's pretty," Maura says about the bride who's on the screen now. "But that dress—I don't know—she can do better."

"Totally agree," Katherine says after a sip of soda.

It's funny because we're not even doing anything that exciting. We're just sitting here watching some show that I'd never choose to watch on my own. But it's relaxed and fun. I'm not stressing about what I'm going to say. Or stressing about what I'm not saying.

"That's gonna be you and Ross when you get married," Trisha says to me. "Ha, ha."

She's referring to this cheesy couple who are meeting with the wedding planner and seem so blissfully in love.

"Yeah, right." I laugh. I keep thinking about what Chelsea said on the phone before, about how I should call him. Chelsea knows what she's talking about when it comes to this kind of stuff. I should listen to her. I should call him, especially when I have the support of the Acceptables around me.

We spend the next few hours watching episode after episode of this stupid show, saying that each couple on the screen is actually someone from our school.

"That's so what Maria Penso's gonna be like!" Trisha shouts. "She's such the diva!"

We go into Maura's kitchen for drop-and-bake chocolate chip cookies. I will call Ross as soon as we're done eating the cookies—that's what I tell myself over and over again. I'm sitting on one of the high wooden stools when I feel my phone vibrating.

I take it out and look at it.

It's Ross.

"Who's calling you?" Katherine asks.

"Um . . . Ross." I smile. I don't know if I should answer or not. I was supposed to call him. I guess it's better this way. But I just keep staring it, looking at it ringing, not answering it.

"Get it! Duh!" Trisha yells. She leans over and pushes the green answer button for me. I give her a look like I'm annoyed, but I'm really not.

I turn my back, because I feel weird talking right in front of them. They get the point because a few seconds later, they've left the kitchen.

"Hi," Ross says. "I'm just gonna say this. Okay?"

"Um, okay." I try not to laugh. I feel like I laugh at every single thing Ross says all the time, and I really don't want to.

"I like you. I *think* you like me. So, let's go out."

I peek into the oven to check on the drop-and-bake cookies because it's easier to focus on that than to focus on the fact that Ross just asked me out. "Sounds good to me," I say finally.

"Good."

"Good." I laugh. I can't help it.

"See you in school," he says.

After I hang up, Maura, Katherine, and Trisha come rushing back in, like they were listening at the door.

They come over, and all lean in and hug me. The kitchen smells like freshly baked chocolate chip cookies, and Maura's heated kitchen floor feels so good on my feet.

"You have a boyfriend," Katherine says.

"And it's Ross!" Trisha adds.

"Have a cookie!" Maura says, taking the tray out of the oven.

We all crack up.

As we're eating cookies and drinking chocolate milk, I decide that they're definitely not the Acceptables.

They're the Favorables now.

32

CHELSEA

Sasha Preston piece of advice: Take the
time to notice improvements in people.

At school on Monday, everyone's talking about Ross
and Dina going out, because apparently he called her over
the weekend. And when I say everyone's talking about it, I
mean everyone that I know. It's like they've never heard of two
people going out before. No one cared this much when I went
out with Pace Lerner. Maybe that's because he moved away a
month later?

Kendall's going on and on about how she realized that
Dina's so cool and how she's like no one else at our school and
how we need to be more open-minded for high school.

And I agree with her.

We're in social studies waiting for class to start when Dina
walks in. I try to see if she looks different, if she has that glow

275

that they say you can get when you're going out with someone. I've never actually seen anyone get it, though. She doesn't. She's still wearing her old jeans and one of her zip-up sweaters. She's like a girl version of Mister Rogers.

Why am I being so mean? It's only inside my head, but still. I wish I could stop.

"Hey," she says, kind of out of breath. She sits down, and a minute later Mr. Valakis calls us over to his desk.

"So we want to have everything set up for the gala a week in advance," he says. "That way the MC of the event can run through everything a few times."

Dina and I look at each other.

"That shouldn't be a problem because you're almost done, yes?" he asks.

We nod but don't say anything.

"So you'll give me the final product on DVD, and I'll make sure to hold on to it until the gala."

We stare at him and still say nothing.

"Okay?"

We nod again, and he gives us a look like he's a little concerned but too tired or uninterested to inquire about it. Then we walk back to our desks.

"What are we gonna do?" I mumble to Dina under my breath.

"No problem. We finish the interviews this week, get all the clips we can, and then I edit it together this weekend." She smiles. "I'm a fast editor. Don't worry."

I know what Ross likes about Dina; she always seems like she has everything under control. It's what always makes me want to call her when my parents are fighting.

She just has a way of making people feel calmer.

"I love the idea about all the interesting facts about everyone," I tell her.

"Me, too. And it's like it was right there in front of us; we just had to see it," she says. "Well, Ross did kind of suggest it. But do you know what I mean?"

"I totally do."

We stay at school really late, and Dina's mom gives me a ride home after what feels like a million more interviews and tons more footage to sort through. I find my mom in the den sorting through files, but she's smiling. "Come sit with me," she says.

So I join her on the couch. "What's for dinner? I'm starving."

"It's a surprise." She smiles even wider and then puts her arm around me. "Actually, go get your shoes on and meet me in the garage."

I look at my watch and realize it's already after seven.

"Where are Alexa and Dad?"

"They'll be there. Don't worry."

I run upstairs, and as I'm getting my shoes on I notice that the first flakes of snow are falling. It's December and we haven't had snow yet.

There's something about a fresh coat of snow that makes everything feel fresh and clean, like a brand-new start, like everything that's under the snow is done and buried and forgotten and by the time the snow melts, spring will be here and it really will be a new beginning.

I wonder why dinner is a surprise, but dinner surprises in my family are rarely bad things, so I'm not worried. And we're going out to eat on a weeknight like we used to, which feels good and exciting and reassuring.

I decide to text Dina:

> sooooo excited about the project now. we have to tell sasha preston. wanna come over friday night? just to hang out?

She writes back a few seconds later:

> I know. I am excited too! Friday sounds good!

I waited so long to have people over this year, but now I feel like I can. Or maybe I just feel like I can have Dina over because she's not going to judge me, because even if my parents get into a fight, so what? I bet she'll have some insightful thing to say about it. Maybe her parents fight, too. Who knows?

I'm in the car with my mom, and she has the oldies station on and she's singing along, and I realize it's the first time I've heard her sing in a while.

I don't know where we're going, but I don't ask. It's kind of nice not knowing for once, and it's not the bad kind of not knowing, where you're all nervous and tense. It's the good kind, where you know something good is about to happen.

We pull into the parking lot, and of course I know where I am now—Riverbay—my family's favorite restaurant. I'm going to get the salmon scampi pasta, and Alexa will get the filet of sole sandwich, and maybe my parents will share two dishes. But the rolls are the best part. They're always warm and freshly baked, and the butter always melts on them perfectly.

Alexa and my dad are already sitting at a table when we walk in, and there are two bouquets of flowers on the table. One of yellow roses and one of pink roses.

"I have some good news," my dad says, smiling like he hasn't smiled in a year. Maybe more. "Ready?"

Alexa finishes buttering her roll, takes a bite, and then says, "Ready."

We all laugh.

"Well, as you may have guessed by the fact that we're out

at Riverbay . . ." He pauses, smiling. "I got a new job. And not just any job. I'll be structuring deals and solving complicated tax issues—all the stuff I really love."

He goes on for a few more minutes, using words and expressions that only my mom understands, but right now I don't even care about understanding what he's saying. I'm just enjoying how happy he looks.

My mom raises her glass of red wine, and Alexa raises her Sprite, and I raise my lemonade, and we all clink glasses.

We eat a delicious meal and even get ice cream sundaes for dessert. And we drive home and there's no fighting, and there's no fighting when we get home, either, and for the first time in months and months, I fall asleep without my headphones.

There's no noise that I need to drown out.

The world is calm and peaceful and happy. At least, my world is, and I'm so grateful. Money doesn't fix everything, but it does mean you can pay bills and buy groceries, so it's pretty important.

The thing is, the other stuff—the fancy jeans and the cars and all of that—it isn't important. It's just stuff, extra stuff, that makes people competitive and mean and angry when they don't have it.

I'm glad my dad has a job now and that he'll be busy and working and out of his workout clothes. But it doesn't mean I'm going to jump right back to insisting on having limited-edition jeans.

33

DINA

Video tip: If you're ending something
on a music cue, bring the music up,
and then fade it out.

We finish our last round of interviews, and it's more
of the same stuff—students who feel like outsiders, students
who want to be recognized for their talents, lots of people who
want the whole being-chipped thing to be abolished.

We're at Chelsea's house, and we're looking through all the
footage, and I'm editing it together on her dad's Mac. We got
an interview with every kid in our grade, and each one said an
interesting fact about himself or herself.

The facts range from "I can eat a whole pizza in fifteen
minutes" to "I play the flute" to "I'm part Native American."

"Isn't it funny how this is so not what we planned to do for
this?" I ask Chelsea.

She nods. "Yeah, and it's not cheesy. It's like we're making our point, but not hitting people over the head with it. You know what I mean?"

"And it's almost unanimous," I add, looking down at the piece of paper with the tally. "People hate chipping."

"It's called 'being chipped'!" Chelsea yells, and laughs. "But yeah, only three people said they liked it, and I think they were being sarcastic."

As I'm editing, I see the clips of the Favorables. Maura saying how she can make the best cheesecake in all of New York State. Katherine saying how she can type faster with one hand than most people can with two. And Trisha saying how she can peel a clementine all in one piece.

They're not boring like I thought they were. They're just regular girls who have unique things to say but never really felt like they could.

"I figured out how we can include Sasha!" Chelsea says, looking over all the footage on the computer. "We can have her do a little introduction."

Chelsea grabs a piece of paper and a pen and quickly writes something down. She hands it to me to read.

Some people felt like outsiders looking in. Some people were seen as insiders but didn't feel that way. Some felt angry. Others felt sad. But what we really learned was that everyone had something to offer. Here are the faces and voices of Rockwood Hills Middle School's eighth graders.

All different. All accepted. All cool.

"That is so good!" I high-five her. "You're such a good writer. I didn't know that!"

She smiles. "Maybe that's my thing?"

"Yeah! *You* should be the one saying that. You can introduce the video," I tell her. "It'll mean so much coming from you."

Chelsea gives me a look. "Come on."

"No, I mean it."

"Fine, but we have to incorporate Sasha in another way then," she says.

"She'll be the last student! The last one, at the end." I jump up onto Chelsea's leather couch. "It'll be perfect."

So I take a break from the editing and e-mail Sasha.

Hi Sasha,

Can you believe it? Our video is almost done. We just need one more thing from you—if you can. Would you video yourself just saying your name and an interesting fact about yourself? We want to put you at the end. We literally taped every single kid in our grade saying their name and an interesting fact. They're all different—some are funny—some are serious. We think it's going to be great.

Thanks!

Dina & Chelsea

"We're waiting for one finishing touch," I tell Mr. Valakis at school on Monday. We just showed him the video, and he seems perplexed but pleased. "But we still have a few days so once I get it, I can finish it, and then bring the final thing to the gala."

"It's very interesting, girls," he says. "I have to be honest, if you had told me you were going to go in this direction, I wouldn't have thought it would work. But it does. And everyone wants to see themselves on screen. And being recognized for something they're proud of—even better." He pauses. "Even if Colby Flarrety is proud of being able to burp the alphabet."

We laugh.

"Good job, girls. Really and truly, a job well done." He shakes our hands. "And I'm excited to see what the finishing touch is."

Chelsea and I look at each other like we're debating if we should tell him or not.

"We want you to be surprised," Chelsea says.

He agrees.

Chelsea and I walk to the cafeteria together. "We did it," I say. "Mr. Valakis likes it. We finished the video! And we even have a few days until the event."

She smiles and stops walking. "You did it, Dina." She nibbles the corner of her mouth. "You were the one who cared about it, who thought about it, who found Sasha. You were the one who continued to work on it even after I was a total you-know-what."

I don't know what to say, because what she's saying is true. Yes, it was what I had to do. But it's also what I wanted to do. "I felt like we could say something with this video, make things better," I add. "And I knew I couldn't be the only one who hated being chipped and didn't feel accepted. I felt like we could make the video mean something to people. And so we did."

We get to the cafeteria and part ways. It's not like I'm just going to sit at Chelsea's table. I don't even want to. That's a big thing that's changed, I guess. I like the people I'm friends with.

I get to the Favorables table and tell them about Mr. Valakis. "He likes the video," I say. "He's actually happy with it. Can you believe it?"

"Yeah." Katherine laughs. "You're good at that stuff. That's, like, your interesting thing."

I smile. "Yeah. You're right."

We eat our sandwiches and talk about tests coming up. No one brings up Chelsea. After that day when everyone was waiting to be interviewed and Chelsea declared that her life wasn't perfect, the Favorables stopped talking about her.

"Hey, girls," we hear someone say, and obviously everyone knows who it is without even looking. My back is to him, so I turn around and smile. He pulls up a chair.

"So, what's going on?" he asks the table, not only me. I think that's nice. A boy should care about a girl's friends, not just the girl he likes.

"Just bugging out about the math test, as per use," Trisha says.

"As per use?" Ross makes fun of Trisha's crazy abbreviation, and we all crack up.

"I'm tempted to do that thing where people store formulas in their calculators," Trisha adds.

Ross makes a face at her and then looks over at me. "She'd never cheat."

"I know."

So we sit there talking, and it feels totally calm and normal. The Favorables haven't fainted because Ross is at their table or anything. I didn't really expect them to, but given the way they acted at the beginning of the year, it could have happened.

Ross stays at our table for the rest of lunch, and we walk out of the cafeteria together like a real couple.

You'd think the whole Ross thing would be what I'm most excited about. But for some reason it's not. It's like a piece of a puzzle—a very, very important piece. But not the only piece.

CHELSEA

Sasha Preston piece of advice: At an exciting event,
step back for a moment and take it all in.

The day of the fiftieth-anniversary celebration, my
mom is happier than I've seen her in weeks. She's getting
decked out in her new dress. It's navy, because she swears
everyone else will be in black and she does not want to be like
everyone else. She even got her hair done for the occasion.

We get to the Country Club and there are a million cars
in the parking lot. The Country Club looks as beautiful as I've
ever seen it, since it's all decorated for the holidays, with tiny
white lights everywhere.

Inside, the parents are milling about, sipping drinks and
eating appetizers with tiny napkins. The teachers look so
different in fancy dresses and suits, and it's almost hard to
recognize them.

The students are all dressed up, too, hanging out in a separate room with a buffet and music. Once everything gets going, we'll all be in the main room together.

A few people will be making welcoming remarks, and then it's time for our video! The thing that will kick off the event!

Dina texts me and we meet by the stage. When I get there, she and Ross are standing together and they look really happy. I never thought Ross could be with someone like Dina, someone who doesn't care about fancy stuff, who doesn't get manicures with her mom, who spends more time pondering life than pondering her wardrobe. But it's like they bring out the best in each other.

These thoughts are so totally cheesy and I'd never say them out loud to anyone, but seeing them together just makes me happy. Dina had to have a first boyfriend sooner or later, and who better for a first boyfriend than Ross Grunner?

Ross is wearing dress pants and a sports jacket and a tie, and I can tell he's wearing cologne.

"Who has the disc?" he asks.

"I do." I reach into my bag and hand it to him.

"Okay, follow me," he says. He's volunteering, helping with all the tech stuff for the event. Mr. Valakis told us to give the final video to Ross and have him make sure it's all in place in the DVD player before the ceremony starts.

Dina grabs my hand and squeezes it, and I feel calmer right away. She always makes me feel calmer, and I wonder how she's able to stay so calm herself or if she's just acting like she's calm.

"Girls, you're all set?" Mr. Valakis asks. "Ross, thanks for being our resident tech expert. Texpert, you could say." He laughs and then leaves the stage.

Finally, it's time.

Ross stays backstage so he can help with the microphones and lights and sound equipment, and Dina and I go to the back, where all the other kids are.

Kendall and Molly are in matching little black dresses, but they swear they didn't plan it.

"We didn't," Molly whines.

Dina and I laugh. We're laughing at her, but I don't know if Molly can tell. And I don't really care.

All of a sudden, I notice that the room is totally quiet and everyone's turned toward the back, to where we're standing. I have no idea what's going on, but it feels like something's coming, like a billion balloons are about to drop from the ceiling.

Then I feel a tap on my shoulder, and I turn around and I see what's going on.

"Sasha!" I scream.

"I had to come," she says. "I know I e-mailed my clip, but I wanted to be here."

Everyone's standing around, staring at her, and it's so crazy because Sasha looks so beautiful and amazing but also like a regular person, just hanging at this celebration.

She stands with us when the event starts and Mr. Oliver, the principal, comes to the microphone on the stage. Dina squeezes my hand—this is happening. This is really happening! I think back to that first day, when I laughed at Dina and got forced to do this, when Kendall and Molly didn't include me in their group and everything seemed so messed up.

I never expected that I'd feel good about things when we got to this point.

"Welcome, everyone, to Rockwood Hills Middle School's fiftieth-anniversary gala!" Mr. Oliver yells, and I swear this is as animated as I've ever seen the man. "We're so happy you're here! All the teachers and the eighth graders have worked so hard to make this night possible. We know you're excited to view the science fair and catch some of the debate tournament, and to listen to the chorus serenade us, and to talk and enjoy each other's company. So, without further ado, please turn your attention to a brief video that two of our eighth graders have made."

It opens with a bang: "Be True to Your School" by the

Beach Boys, with shots of kids in the hallways, the cafeteria, at their lockers talking with one another, and with the other footage we got in the beginning, when we really had no idea what we were going to do.

And then it goes into my introduction to the video and the thing about everyone being different and cool. It's weird to see myself up there. But it's good, too, because I feel like I've done something. For the first time, I feel like I didn't just sit here and go along and have people see me the way they wanted to see me. For the first time, I feel like I made a difference and said what I wanted to say.

And when the video's playing, everyone's cheering, and not just for their friends—everyone's cheering for everyone. Even Christine Whitmore and her thing about the T-shirts, and Paul Bellogs and his thing about arriving at school at exactly 7:43 every single day. And even the more common ones, like Drew Phillips loving to play guitar—people still cheer and clap.

The parents are happy to see their kids, and the kids are happy to see themselves and their friends.

And at the end, the surprise part: Sasha.

"I'm Sasha Preston," she says. "And I'm proud to be an alumna of Rockwood Hills Middle School." She pauses and smiles. "And from now on: no one gets chipped!"

After she says that, everyone's yelling "Yeah!" and cheering so loud—louder than I've ever heard them cheer before. And it feels like some kind of private joke that only the kids in the room know about. Even though being chipped is a bad thing, right now it seems funny, and unique, and special to this school.

When the video ends, Mr. Oliver smiles and says, "It's a special place. And there's something you all should know: it's only getting better."

There's lots of applause after that, and Mr. Oliver tells everyone about the events for the rest of the night.

Dina and I look at each other.

"I'm sad it's over," I tell her.

"Me, too," she says. "But it was good, wasn't it?"

I nod. "Definitely."

I feel a tap on my shoulder and turn around.

"So this is what you were working on in the library all these weeks," library helper says, and as he's talking, I finally remember his name. Sebastian. Such an awesome name.

"Yeah, pretty good, huh?"

"It was awesome," he says.

"You haven't been in the library in a long time," I say, and then realize that sounds a little stalker-ish.

"Yeah, I finished my community-service hours," he says.

"Guess you'll have to find me in other parts of the school."

We both crack up.

"I'm gonna go get some more soda," Sebastian says. "See you in a bit."

I turn back to Dina, and she's standing there smiling at me like she totally knows what's going on, that I had a tiny crush on Sebastian this whole time even though we didn't talk at all and I couldn't even remember his name.

We all spend the rest of the night dancing and eating and visiting the science fair and the debate team and watching the improv troupe.

Dina has her video camera, of course, documenting the whole thing, and when I see her doing that now, I don't think it's weird. I think it's cool. There are things you want to remember and record, because if you don't, you'll forget them or you'll remember them differently from how they actually were. There are moments you want to capture just as they are.

"You're going to think I'm such a video nerd for saying this, but I'm going to say it anyway," Dina starts, after she takes a sip of her Shirley Temple. "Sometimes in order to really see things, you just have to look through a different lens."

I grab a few mini hot dogs off the tray. "I don't think you're a video nerd," I say. "I think you're right."

And I really, really mean that.

ACKNOWLEDGMENTS

I owe oodles of gratitude to: Dave, Mom, Dad, David, Max, Heidi, Aunt Emily, Aaron, Karen, and the rest of the Rosenbergs, Libby Isaac, the Indiana relatives, Shark Attack, the BWL Library team, and every single girl who has written me an e-mail or a real letter.

"Thank you" doesn't seem like enough for Alyssa Eisner Henkin, the best agent in the history of the world, but I will say "Thank you" anyway. To everyone at Abrams and Amulet, especially Susan, Howard, Jason, Chad, Jim, Mary Ann, Laura, and Elisa: you all make the most beautiful books, and I am so lucky to be a part of that.

Maggie Lehrman, thank you for making me work so hard and for putting so much of yourself into my books. I owe you something huge, and I will send it along as soon as I figure out what it is.

Finally, to my little Aleah Violet: thank you for being you.

Lisa Greenwald is the author of *My Life in Pink & Green*, *My Summer of Pink & Green*, and *Sweet Treats & Secret Crushes*. She works in the library at the Birch Wathen Lenox School on the Upper East Side of Manhattan. She is a graduate of the New School's MFA program in writing for children and lives in Brooklyn, New York. Visit her online at www.lisagreenwald.com.

This book was designed

by Chad W. Beckerman. The text is set in 12-point Adobe Garamond, a typeface based on those created in the sixteenth century by Claude Garamond. Garamond modeled his typefaces on ones created by Venetian printers at the end of the fifteenth century. The modern version used in this book was designed by Robert Slimbach, who studied Garamond's historic typefaces at the Plantin-Moretus Museum in Antwerp, Belgium. The display type is Hollywood Deco.

KEEP READING FOR A SNEAK PEEK AT
LISA GREENWALD'S NEXT BOOK,
THE SEQUEL TO *MY LIFE IN PINK & GREEN*

My Summer of Pink & Green

Lucy's tip for a great summer:
Appreciate every moment.
Summer is fleeting and goes by fast!

School got out a week ago, but it doesn't feel like summer yet. It will soon, though. As soon as Claudia drives up and gets out of the car and runs to hug me, then it will feel like summer. The best feeling in the whole, entire world.

"It's gonna be a Jetta," Yamir says. "College kids always drive Jettas." We're sitting on my front porch drinking my mom's famous homemade mint iced tea: me; my best friend, Sunny Ramal; her brother, Yamir; and our friend Evan. He's pretty much Sunny's boyfriend, but we're all friends with him too. The others always turn their noses up at the mint iced tea, but once it's in the special tall glasses with little pieces of mint floating on the top, they can't resist. It's just too refreshing.

"I don't think so; Jettas are fancy, aren't they?" I ask. We're guessing cars because Claudia's driving home with a friend from school. If Claudia were flying home from Chicago, we'd pick her up at the airport and I'd even make one of those name signs that professional drivers use. But she got a ride home instead. Mom and Grandma were all worried about the long drive, and they insisted that she stop and stay overnight somewhere. Her friend Lauren is the one driving her; she lives in Fairfield, which is like an hour from here.

"It's gonna be some old car," Sunny says, standing up. She wants to be the first one to see Claudia coming, but I don't see how that's going to happen if we don't even know what car she's coming in.

"No way," I add. "Girls named Lauren don't have beat-up old cars. Maybe a Honda, but a new one."

"Maybe it's a motorcycle!" Evan shouts. "Wouldn't that be hilarious?"

I give him a stare-down. "No, Evan Mass, it would not be hilarious, because my mom and grandma would probably pass out from shock. Then we'd have to take them to the hospital." I keep up my stare-down. If he's going to be my best friend's boyfriend, then he can't say dumb things like that. "Motorcycles are really dangerous, you know."

He cracks up, and Sunny and Yamir do too.

I don't see what's so funny. "They are. I'm serious."

Sunny pats my knee. "He was just kidding, Lucy."

Thankfully my mom comes out with a tray holding a full pitcher of more mint iced tea and a bowl of strawberries and breaks the tension. "Hungry?" she asks. When none of us answer, she says, "You know, you guys can go swimming. I'm sure Claudia will come on back when she gets here."

The pool! OK, I changed my mind. It will really feel like summer when we're all in the pool. Claudia will probably run inside and throw on her favorite red-and-white gingham bikini and then she'll race out to join us. We'll have diving contests and make Sunny be the judge. She always gives me a ten. And we'll go down the spiral slide a billion times. Sometimes I even sit on Claudia's lap when we go down the spiral slide. It makes Grandma nervous, but we do it anyway.

Claudia's friends will come over and BBQ like crazy—Grandma always lets them use the grill even though she says I'm not old enough. They'll make hamburgers and hot dogs, and portobello burgers for their vegetarian friends. They'll hang out for hours, and they'll let me hang out with them too, some of the time.

It will feel like summer will last forever, and I'll keep telling myself that it won't last forever but that I need to appreciate it and savor every second: every sip of Mom's iced tea, every trip down the spiral slide, every diving contest.

"She's here!" I scream. I know it's her because the windows are rolled down and her head is out the front passenger side like she's a golden retriever.

They pull into the driveway.

"A Subaru!" Yamir says. "We should have known. College kids always drive Subarus."

I don't even care to discuss with him about how he knows that. I'm too excited to see Claudia, to give her hugs, to talk to her about everything—especially the opening of the spa—that I just don't have time to deal with Yamir.

He's been so weird lately. He doesn't get why it's such a big deal that Claudia's coming home. He takes it for granted that his sister is home all the time, but I haven't seen Claudia since September, since she didn't come home for Thanksgiving. Then she was in El Salvador over winter break, and she went to Ghana for spring break. For an eighteen-year-old, she travels a lot.

I run over to the car and Claudia hops out and we hug for a million years like I thought we would. "I missed you so much," I whisper in her ear.

"I missed you too, Luce!"

Her friend Lauren starts unloading the trunk and I'm thankful that Yamir goes over to help. He can be a gentleman sometimes, but then other times he can act like a complete doofus. Grandma says that's just how boys his age act. But I don't really believe her—can't he just act nicer? For me?

"These are yours, right, Claud?" Lauren asks her, holding up a duffel. Claudia looks over, and that's when I notice that there's another person here. A tall, skinny guy, standing right near the car talking to Evan about the Subaru's muffler or something.

"Yeah, those are mine. Bean's are the ones in the backseat."

"Bean is here?" I ask without thinking.

Claudia does a head-jerk motion in his direction, trying to get his attention, and he comes over to where we're standing. I look around for Mom and Grandma. The moment we've all been waiting for—Claudia coming home—is finally here!

"You must be Lucy," this Bean guy says, with a hand up to high-five me.

"I am." I smile and high-five him back. "And you must be Bean? Well, duh, I mean I know you're Bean, Claudia just said that. But I remember your name. Claudia said you helped look over the grant application a few months ago."

"I did. I did." He nods like he's so proud of himself. "I'm pre-law."

"Huh?"

"It means he's going to be a lawyer, Lucy," Claudia explains.

I feel stupid. I could have figured that out.

"But it's a dual major with the business school," Bean adds.

I nod. Bean sounds like he's on a job interview. I'm not really concerned with his major right now. It's summer! He shouldn't be thinking about school anyway.

"Welcome home!" Mom yells, running outside, a dish towel over her right shoulder. "Ma, Claudia's home!" she yells back into the house.

A few seconds later, Grandma comes out, and then we're all together. I don't even realize that Sunny, Yamir, and Evan went back onto the porch until I hear the click of Yamir's iPhone camera taking a picture of all of us standing around in the driveway.

"Such a photo op," he says with a grin. "Right, Luce-Juice? You're all about the photo ops, especially one like this."

Sometimes I feel like Yamir knows the right thing to do and he does it, but then he says something obnoxious while doing it, and that takes all the goodness out of it.

"Thanks." I put my hand on my hip and go into a model pose and he snaps another shot.

"So, Mom, Grandma," Claudia starts. "This is my friend Lauren, and this is Bean."

I wonder why Claudia doesn't refer to Bean as her friend.

"Lovely to meet you, thank you for driving her home, Lauren," Grandma says. "You probably want to get going. I bet your parents are worried sick about you doing so much driving and all the crazies on the road."

"Grams, it's OK." Claudia pats her shoulder. "She's meeting them nearby, and then they're going to their beach house in Newport for the summer."

"That's lovely," Mom says. Everything's lovely, apparently.

I'm still standing there, wondering if it's too soon to go change into bathing suits and jump in the pool. I wish Lauren and Bean would just leave already so I could have Claudia to myself.

"What a lovely tote," Mom says about this long bag that Lauren has over her shoulder. It's just a canvas tote with the word *Tranquility* embroidered in pink letters. It's nothing that special, really.

"Thanks. It's from Etsy." Lauren smiles. "It's basically the only place I shop these days."

"Oh, I know," Mom says. "It's just so fabulous that artists can sell directly to—"

"So, Mom, Grandma, Lucy," Claudia interrupts, thankfully, because this conversation about Lauren's tote bag was getting really boring for everyone except Lauren and Mom.

"I invited Bean to come stay with us for the summer."

I gasp. I feel like someone sucked all the water out of our perfect pool with a straw and there will never be water in it again. Everything I had been looking forward to just evaporated.

TO BE CONTINUED . . .

KEEP READING!

FROM THE AUTHOR OF *MY LIFE IN PINK & GREEN*
LISA GREENWALD
Sweet Treats & Secret Crushes

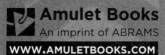

Amulet Books
An imprint of ABRAMS
WWW.AMULETBOOKS.COM

Send author fan mail to:
Amulet Books, Att: Marketing, 115 West 18th Street, New York, NY 10011
Or e-mail marketing@abramsbooks.com. All mail will be forwarded.

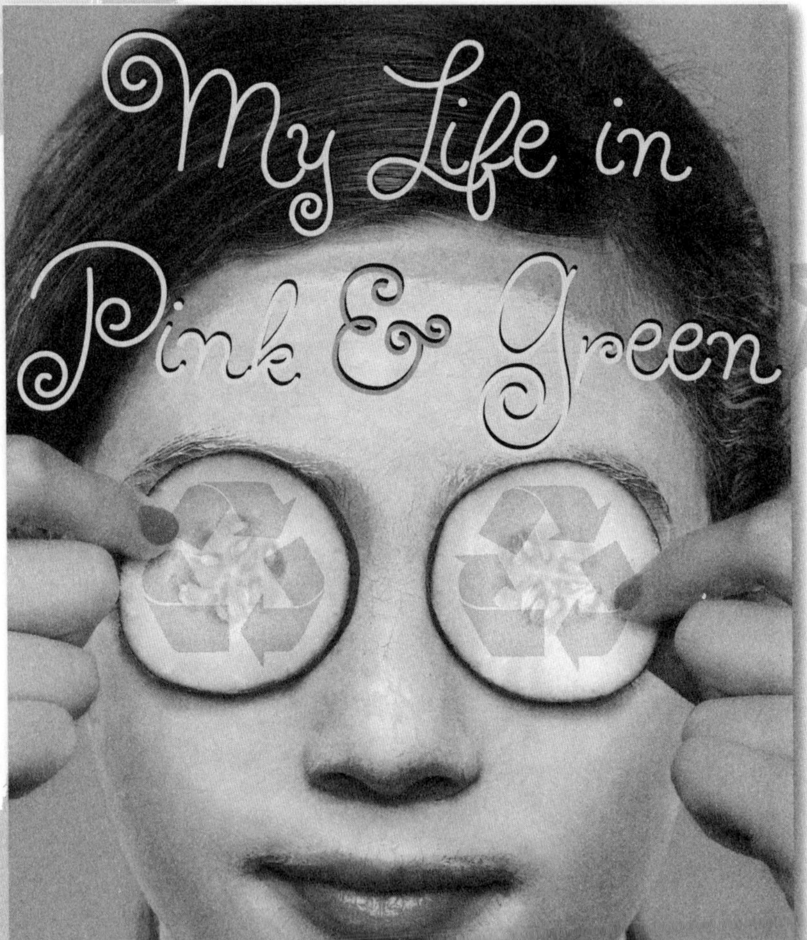
My Life in Pink & Green
LISA GREENWALD

SEQUEL TO *MY LIFE IN PINK & GREEN*

My Summer of Pink & Green

LISA GREENWALD